BARBARA WILLARD

The Gardener's Grandchildren

Illustrations by Gordon King

McGRAW-HILL BOOK COMPANY

New York   St. Louis   San Francisco

Library of Congress Cataloging in Publication Data

Willard, Barbara.
The gardener's grandchildren.
SUMMARY: Two children become curious about the
departure of their grandfather's employer, who left
their "Garden Island" off Scotland years ago after
instructing the gardener to faithfully keep the island
beautiful until his return.
[1.   Mystery and detective stories.   2.   Islands—
Fiction]   I.   Title.
PZ7.W6547Gar   [fic]   78-23637
ISBN 0-07-070291-8

First published and distributed in the United States of America
by McGraw-Hill Book Company, 1979.

123456789 MUMU 7832109

THE GARDENER'S GRANDCHILDREN

INNIS GHARAIDH

GARDEN ISLAND

Ella had a new dress, but it was black, so there was no great pleasure to be had from it. 'Take what you need from the house,' Mr Alexander had said, when he went away from the island years ago. Ella knew about that, but she had never been told why he went; it was a subject that had become encrusted with secrecy – like some old box lying in a cobwebby attic. Often and often she and Rob spoke of it, wondering, making wild guesses, never knowing if they were anywhere near the truth. Why did he go? More importantly, when would he come back? Ever?

In spite of its owner's instructions that they should take anything they needed, the house was entered only to be cleaned. Then doors and windows stood open to sun and sea, wind and frost, and Ella's mother went through the rooms like a whirlwind; but a solemn whirlwind, for this house, like the island itself, was a trust to be honoured if need be to the end of time. Sometimes Ella went with her mother to the house and helped a bit, but was never allowed to open or touch or peer – there were many tempting boxes and caskets and she longed to see inside. The house, however, was by now a sleeping house, and even when Ella and her mother were there, it barely stirred. Everything remained as it had been left, whatever was moved was carefully replaced. If the Laird should return unexpectedly he was to see at once that he had come home to what he remembered. Till now, only books had been borrowed.

Then, when the black dress was needed, the long habit was

broken. After much consultation between the children's mother and their grandfather, Ella was taken by her mother up to Mrs Alexander's bedroom. After trying several keys on the heavy bunch of all sizes, Ella's mother unlocked the enormous wardrobe and stood back with Ella at her side.

'Poor soul,' Margaret Ross said, soft and sighing.

There hung Mrs Alexander's clothes, that had not been touched since she died – long before Mr Alexander went away, before Ella was born, even. A great smell of camphor drifted out into the room, too intense for any moth or mouse to have braved, even for this horde of delicious food and bedding – cloth coats with fur collars, tailor-mades of fine tweed, lace-trimmed gowns, flowers of silk and satin, hats with plumes and curling feathers; ribbon sashes, hung in a bunch, gloves long and short, of kid or fur; shawls fine as cobweb, shoes and slippers, boots, parasols ... The doors flung open stirred the garments hanging there. Mysteriously, a button fell and bounced from the wardrobe's edge to the carpet at Ella's feet. She jumped and stepped back, looking down at the button in concern, not knowing whether to pick it up, glancing sideways at her mother.

'This skirt will do very well,' Mrs Ross was murmuring, delicately shifting the folds of one garment from the folds of another, taking the skirt from its place with an air of apology. 'No touching!' she said sharply, as Ella, having picked up the button, sought to replace it. Between them they set up a draught that stirred the clothes yet again, and there came on the still and airless air a shower of particles, minute shreds of feather from a tasselled boa, a breath of lace fragments, a fall of tiny beads from the bodice of an evening gown.

Ella stood almost frozen, her shoulders hunched, half expecting every garment in the great cupboard to shiver and fall, to blow out all over the room, draping their remnants about her head and shoulders, filling her mouth, muffling and blinding her ...

'There now!' said her mother, both vexed and sad. And she gently shut the door, turning the key almost silently. She put her arm around Ella's shoulders and seemed to urge her from the room – almost as if she, too, had felt that strange threat.

'Should we find something for Rob?' asked Ella, recovering. 'Could you maybe choose him something of Mr Alexander's?'

'No, no. We should not do so. Mrs Alexander is long dead, poor thing. But Mr Alexander is still living and will need his things again. We would know if it were otherwise.'

They went from the house and it was left to sleep again. Again Mrs Ross turned a key on the great bunch; though there was none on the island now but herself and her father and her two children.

On the day of the funeral Rob was buttoned into his one good suit, which had belonged to another lad before him and was already too tight, with a black bow tied under his stiff round collar and a wide black band on his sleeve. It was a warm day and already, as the boat made its way to the mainland for the funeral, his face looked sticky. Neither Ella nor Rob had ever been to a funeral and first occasions hold a hidden excitement; but since the funeral was their father's they knew they must not enjoy it, though they had never known him very well or liked him very much. For them he had been a man of black looks and hard punishment. He had been a friendless man altogether, unsmiling, lacking any understanding of his children since he had forgotten entirely that he had once been a child himself – he might almost have denied the enactment of his own childhood, so completely had it passed from his understanding. It was their grandfather the brother and sister loved best in all the world, and next his daughter, their mother ... Oh poor father! Ella thought now. Even his own children had not wanted to be his friends ... Then tears filled her eyes. They were tears of shame for what she had failed to offer him, they were not tears of sorrow for his going. They were not real tears at all; she was able to blink them away before even one could be squeezed out properly.

There were three boats crossing to the mainland. The first carried the coffin; Ian and Tam Dougal at the oars, the

7

Minister, Mr Grant, in the bows. He had come to the island to meet and greet the living and the dead, and to escort the coffin to its resting place. The second boat was towed behind the first. Had Mr Alexander been at home he would undoubtedly have sat alone in this second boat, rowed, perhaps, by one of the Maclean boys. It had seemed right to the widow that her husband's absent employer should be at least represented. Grand folk, she knew, quite often sent their empty carriages to follow funerals, even though they might excuse their own attendance.

In the third boat, the family was rowed by Alister Maclean. Rob sat with his grandfather, Ella sat beside her mother. On Margaret Ross's far side sat Alister's stepmother, who had been Lizzie Best, Mr Alexander's housekeeper. Although she was a southerner, she had stayed on after Mr Alexander left, and she was the only member of the mainland community with whom the island family maintained any kind of relationship. When Lizzie Best – for so she would always be to them – heard of Wallace Ross's death, she had had Alister row her at once to the island, that she might take her condolences to the widow. She took also her own black bonnet and veil as a loan.

'You are a kind soul, Lizzie,' Ella had heard her mother say. But she had accepted the bonnet with hardly concealed distaste, and wore it now as if it burnt her to the skull.

As the boats rounded the headland and took the wind off the open sea, the church appeared to rise up on the cliff top ahead with a new importance, as if it had been specially erected for this occasion. The shape of the cliff itself always amazed Ella and Rob – you could see plainly that the island had been broken off the mainland one day, like a piece broken off a large cake; and if the sea had not nibbled at both edges, the island might almost have been fitted back into place . . . Someone must have been watching from the church tower, for immediately the bell tolled once. As if released by the sound, the Minister gave up his silence, praying loudly and with great determination, as if for all of them.

Everyone suddenly sat up and braced himself for what was

ahead. Ella looked at her mother. Mrs Ross had straightened her back and lifted her chin. She was always pale, but today it was as if her skin had never known the healthy bloom of summer sunshine. It seemed to be stretched tightly over her bones, shining, not damply, but with a strange polished look, like pale marble, as if the bones had risen to the surface of her face.

Ella moved a shade closer, so that she felt her mother's shoulder against her own cheek, and how the muscles were rigid as rods all the way down to the tight-clasped hands in their black gloves. Ella wished she might speak, but silence had settled on them all before ever they got into the boats, and now even Mr Grant's voice, at its energetic praying, seemed out of place. Her mother, as if answering, turned her head slowly and looked down at Ella. Her mouth stayed solemn, but her eyes smiled. She unclasped her hands and took Ella's hand on to her knee as if it were some little animal that needed comfort. Ella felt the beautiful darns in the black fingers, and looked forward anxiously to the moment when the gloves would be peeled off and the hands be real hands again.

And then she wondered what she meant by real, by real life as she had known it. Now, for sure, it could only be different. But how?

Then she wondered if Miss Christabel would be in the church ... 'I'll thank you to be off about your own concerns,' her father had said to Miss Christabel, when she came to ask if Ella and Rob might go to the village school, where she was teacher. 'My bairns know their place and I'll see they keep it. They've to work and there'll be little time for your books. They have instruction enough from their grandfather!'

Miss Christabel had flushed the colour of some beautiful peony and walked away stiff-shouldered to the boat she had rowed herself from the mainland ...

The bell sounded again as the boats ran in on the narrow shingly beach. As soon as they grounded, everything became more real – the crunch of feet on the stones, the crying of seagulls disturbed on the cliffs above, the short exchanges

9

between the men. Ella looked after Rob, and he at that very moment, as if she had called him, turned back to her over his shoulder. She thought he looked frightened and she nudged up to him quickly. He was pale, and since he had his mother's dark hair and clear skin, he looked very like her. He was only a year younger than Ella, so she dared not take his hand, as she would have liked to do. She was increasingly sorry for him in his tight suit. Now that they were ashore the breeze was lost to them and the sun struck on their heads as heavily as the single strokes of the mourning bell.

The party began the steep ascent of the cliff, up the narrow path that was dry and crumbly in this season. Ella and Rob came last, for they had hung back together, almost as if they might decide suddenly to run away, to escape the dismal occasion.

Suddenly Ella stopped, so that Rob cannoned into her and had to grab at her to steady himself.

'Where is he?' she said, her eyes wild. 'Where *is* he?'

'Go on,' muttered Rob in a furious voice. 'Will you go *on*, Ella Ross!'

'But where is he? Where's poor father now?'

'In his coffin,' Rob growled.

But it was the coffin Ella had missed. '*Where?*'

'It's the path. Too steep. It was Alister told me. They must bring it up the cliff face with ropes.'

Ella dared not reply – she feared to burst with shrill laughter.

'Get on will you?' Rob growled. 'Granda's waiting.'

There were nine or ten villagers among those now waiting at the gate of the churchyard. Ella looked hopefully for faces to which she could give a name, though she might never have spoken to their owners. She was searching for Miss Christabel. But why indeed should she come to the funeral of a man who had treated her with such insulting rudeness under his own roof? Not even Maggie Ogilvie, the postmistress, was standing there – she at least was one Ella knew a little. She and her brother came seldom to the village, and never alone, standing silent while their mother did her shopping, or their grandfather went to the post office to collect the quarterly letter from the bank, or catalogues of plants that he had sent for. Once, nearly a year ago, Rob had tired of this and had taken the boat and rowed himself across, and learnt more in one afternoon of the mainland community than in the years of his life before. But he had been so severely punished for it that he never did it again ... That must have been the last beating their father had been strong enough to give either of them, Ella thought now, as she stood there knowing that the family was being talked about by the onlookers. The women murmured sympathetically as they stared. A number of children were there, too, looking both inquisitive and righteous – an expression, Ella was sure, that spoke deep scorn of the island children who never went to school.

There was a sudden whispering and straightening. The coffin appeared, borne by Alister and his cousin, Angus Maclean, and by Ian and Tam, who had rowed it across the Sound. The Minister walked ahead, intoning the appropriate psalm about life and death. Ella was seized by the wild fancy that Mr Grant, too, had been hauled up from the bobbing boat by the Dougal brothers, swinging gently round and round, and praying as he came ... She gasped and clapped her hands over her face, in a panic again lest she should laugh, hoping that it must appear as if she were crying or saying her prayers ... And again she thought, *Poor Father! Poor Father!* But this time her eyes stayed empty.

Then they were going into the church, Mother and Granda walking behind the coffin, then Rob and Ella, then those vaguely connected, like Lizzie and Alister and various of their relations; then the rest higgledy-piggledy. Since the church was small they made quite a respectable gathering. Ella looked at the ground as she walked down the aisle, longing for the moment when she might sidle into a pew. Rob pulled her sleeve, but she shook him off. He persisted, and when at last she turned her head he muttered, 'There – there ...'

Ella saw Miss Christabel, her head bent, and there beside her was Maggie Ogilvie, the postmistress, whom she had looked for in vain outside the church. Everything changed for Ella. Poor father's funeral might as well have been a wedding ...

The noon light was slanting dramatically and full of dancing dust as the funeral service began. Outside was the hot, still sunshine, the harvest stooked in those small fields won from rough ground, from a territory mostly given up to sheep. The sheaves stood in rows like warriors, and from their embrace hung wilting poppies. In one of the weather-stunted trees that stood in that high graveyard a blackbird whistled, but lazily, knowing the end of summer was almost come. Ella listened to the bird rather than to the words about death and everlasting life beyond the grave, promises of heaven strangely cancelled by threats of hell. Her spirit seemed to soar far away, caught up on wings of imagination and hope, beguiled by thoughts of the future which now must surely be different from anything she had known.

She came back to reality on the unexpected sound of sobbing. It was not her mother, whose tears were withheld and always would be, but Rob who gave to this occasion its first open sorrow and proper dignity ... It seemed very strange to Ella, who had so often comforted her brother after beatings, risking a box on the ears or the fury and hunger and fright of being locked up in the little room in the roof as a punishment for showing sympathy.

The boy's tears brought others. Eyes were wiped, noses bravely blown. No one had had a good word for Wallace Ross while he lived – yet now his death, or maybe thoughts of the inevitable certainty of their own, distressed them greatly. The whole mood of the congregation changed. It softened and grew warm, and sympathy then overtook self-pity. When it was all over, with Ella walking back down the aisle holding her mother's hand, while Rob walked on the far side, a murmur ran towards them and around them. Poor fatherless bairns ... What might come to them now?

What indeed? As Ella let back into her mind those thoughts of a changed life which she had dutifully banished for the time being, she glanced towards Miss Christabel and met a brief smile, slight, sad, yet encouraging. Wait and see, it seemed to say. It is not to be considered just now. But later ... Be patient. The time shall come ...

'Why did you cry?' Ella asked Rob in a whisper.

He stared back bold and unwinking. 'I did not.'

They were all by then in Lizzie Best's parlour, in the good stone farmhouse of the Macleans, that was dug deep and thick into the ground, with all about it the acres that Lizzie's step-sons doggedly farmed. The funeral party made a great crowd in Lizzie's front parlour, which had never looked finer, for she had draped this and that with black for the occasion. The curtains were tied back with sashes of black cloth; the marble clock that struck above the hearth wore a black bow that had slipped a little to one side, giving it a jaunty air.

At first the guests stood uneasily, almost in silence, or at most speaking in a solemn undertone to the nearest neighbour. But then the food was spread out; cold ham and plum cake, and beverages. For the children, of whom six or seven had tagged along with their parents, there was ginger beer and lemonade. There were not so many sociable occasions that such as this one could fail to supply enjoyment. Gradually in the stuffy heat of the little parlour, the pleasures of gossip, and beverages, they all grew cheerful. If they kept their spirits mildly within bounds out of respect for the bereaved, it was only because they could be certain that on such occasions the bereaved left the party early.

After a while the children drifted all to one corner of the room. Girls perched on the shiny sofa, swinging their legs and tossing their hair; boys leant against the wall in a swaggering manner, downing good draughts of ginger beer and making sure of a helping from any plate that was carried past. Rob and Ella stood close together. Because they were allowed so seldom on the mainland, because they had been kept from going to the school there, they knew as little of these children as they knew of all the rest. The children, however, knew all about Ella and Rob. They were only two to know about, so that was easy – and anyway they listened to their parents' talk.

'I can sit on my hair,' said one girl, throwing her head back and just managing to slide the ends of her fair plaits under her bottom. 'Can you sit on your hair, Ella Ross?'

'You see fine she cannot,' cried the girl's sister. 'Her hair's hardly down to her wee shoulder blades. You're thin as a water-rail, Ella Ross.'

'I am not, so,' said Ella.

'And black as a crow,' said the girl.

'I have my black dress for the funeral,' Ella answered with dignity. 'When you have your father die, you'll maybe have a black dress, too.'

'My father die!' cried the girl. 'I can see that!'

'I'd a black dress for my granny when she died,' said a bigger girl. 'I'd have maybe worn it the day, but I'm grown too tall long since. It'd not be decent.'

'Maybe Ella'll be grown before she needs her black dress next,' said the first girl. Adding, 'Maybe not.'

'When should I need it?' Ella cried, cold in the stuffy room.

The girls turned away, giving little embarrassed laughs, and putting their hands over their mouths. One of the older boys said, but with solemn courtesy, 'It is your Granda they mean. John Maitland is an old man.'

Ella saw Rob bunch his fists and she grabbed at him. But he had swung his arm already, catching the lad on the nose. The victim said nothing, he made no move to strike back. He stood amazed, distressed, a runnel of blood appearing dram-atically from each nostril.

'Mam! Mam!' cried his sister, jumping from the sofa.

'Whisht you, Eileen,' he said, shoving her back roughly. He wiped the blood with the back of his hand, saying sadly and civilly to Ella, 'I meant no harm – no harm at all. Tell him.'

Then with dignity he left them, thrusting his way steadily across the crowded, noisy room. He went outside into the sun-shine and sought a private place where he might recover.

The rest of the children moved away, looking back over their shoulders, pulling faces, making remarks that could only have been rude. Ella and Rob were alone, strange island children unable to communicate with their own kind. They even spoke a little differently, for their grandfather had modelled his own manners on those of the man he had admired so greatly; he spoke with the measured tones he had learnt from Mr Alexander, and, allowing for differences in age, the rest had picked up his pace and his tone. It was only to be expected that such differences should set the island children apart. If only Miss Christabel had been there, she would surely have spoken up for Ella and Rob, but she had gone home after they came from the church, the school being closed for the day, as it was always when any member of that small community died and was seen to his grave.

The afternoon wore away as Ella and Rob sat side by side on the sofa, she wishing for the quicker growing of her reddish hair, he flexing his fists and looking thoughtfully at his knuckles. Then suddenly their grandfather was standing before them, holding out a hand to each, saying quietly, 'There now. It is over. Your mother's weary. We'll away home.'

They looked up at him thankfully. He was smiling. He was short and broad-shouldered, still strong though he was spoken of, and spoke of himself, as an old man. Only a slight shortness of breath, that could take him unawares, betrayed his years. His hair was clear of white, it was dark and thick like his beard, which he wore trimmed square, shaving only his upper lip. Out of his weathered face, over his fine whiskers, his grey eyes looked lovingly into the unhappy faces of his grandchildren. They took the hands he held out. The palms were hard as bone, polished by years of gripping tools, the nails broken short, the fingers ridged from the soil it was his trade and his loving purpose to tame. If he believed himself the best gardener in the world, or at least the best north of the Border, he would never say so. He was a proud man who knew nothing of vanity.

'Come now,' he said again, in his deep soft voice.

He led them across the little room, weaving and edging among the increasingly rowdy guests many of whom did not even see them go. Their mother was outside, sitting alone in the last of the sun. When she saw them she rose, taking off the bonnet Lizzie had lent her, laying it on the sill of the open parlour window from which the merriment gushed in a noisy flood.

'There,' she said, and that was all.

She went away from them down the path and they followed after, leaving the funeral behind for ever, hearing the sound of the piano bounding from the open windows, the real party beginning as the bereaved left for home. They scrambled down to the shore, Rob dragging off his tight jacket as he went. Their boat lay beached and waiting, her name painted along the gunwale – *Ròin*, or *seal*. They had another boat, old, big and ugly, called because of it *Caillich*, meaning *an old woman*; *Caillich* was forever in need of repair. Granda shoved the boat into the shallow water and one by one they climbed in, splashing through the barely stirring tide-edge, reckless of boots and stockings and skirt hems, delighting in that quick cool seeping touch of the sea, in the feeling that somehow they were washing away the day.

With their grandfather pulling out across the Sound, the two children began to smile a little. Their mother at last peeled off her black darned gloves, laying them palm to palm, then folding, then rolling, then turning them back neatly into a ball. Each movement was a tiny step of return to the commonsense matters of everyday. The pins had half fallen out of her dark hair when she took off Lizzie's bonnet, and now she took out the last of them, and shook her head, lifting her face and breathing deeply, so that her hair fell fine and straight down her back. She was not a particularly pretty woman, but Ella thought that now she looked beautiful.

'It is a very fine evening,' she said. 'And tomorrow will be a fine day.'

It was as if she were promising them a happy future, yet somehow Ella experienced a feeling of shock that made her look away. She gazed over the increasing distance of calm water to the mainland. She could just see, on the point that crowned the village, a figure standing solitary. She started and cried out, then bit her lip, feeling foolish. But for a second she had seemed to see her father standing there, and had known that nothing, after all, was changed.

'Who is it?' she cried.

Her mother answered. 'It is the man come to work for the Dougals. Mr Erskine. George Erskine. You have seen him before this, Ella.'

'There must be a man come to work for us, too, Margaret,' her father said, saving Ella a reply. 'We are bound to find another pair of hands. Mr Alexander would wish it.'

'Aye, he would,' Mrs Ross agreed. 'Who knows? George Erskine himself'd maybe think of a change. When the harvest's done, that is.'

'Maybe. Maybe.'

Ella looked quickly at Rob, but immediately he glanced away. Their mother raised her arm.

Far off, the tiny figure seemed to be waving back.

Innis Gharbh, the Rough Island, had been the name of the place before Mr Alexander went to live there. With many other scattered properties it had belonged to his family. In the way of such large landowners they had left it to an agent's care and then all but forgotten its existence. When the agent died he was not replaced and so things remained until, on the death of Mr Alexander's father, it was rediscovered along with other half-forgotten parcels of land. From the first moment of visiting this part of his inheritance, Mr Alexander had conceived the idea of a great garden. So, when the dream became a reality, the name of the island was changed gradually when it was spoken of on the mainland – there they called it, a little contemptuously, Innis Gharaidh, the Garden Island.

William Hamilton Alexander was rich, the only son of a man who had left his native Scotland as a young man to make a great fortune overseas, neglecting his own inheritance to do so. His son did not care to recall the labouring thousands who had sweated to produce the wealth that had now become his. He spent it freely, even wildly, on beautiful things; as if by doing so he somehow improved the quality of this questionable gold.

'A great man would maybe have given away every penny,' their grandfather had once said to Ella and Rob. And he reminded them of the rich young man in the Bible. 'The Laird would never claim to be a great man. But in every sort and sense of the word, he is a good man.'

So in his young manhood, all those years ago, Mr Alexander had returned to the land that bred his forefathers, and parting with all his other properties had made his home on this least part of his inheritance, setting himself the long rough task of making it beautiful. The house, once a poor crofter's home, he had made four times its size. He had filled it with fine furniture and pictures, with glass and porcelain and rich carpets. He had laboured in the garden as hard and as long as he believed men had laboured for his father. He tussled with the rocks, hewing them to the shape he desired, and fought with the lush growth of briar and broom, of whins and heather and tangling honeysuckles, which flourished because of the island's situation. Though it faced out to sea, it was held in the graceful arms of the Sound and sheltered to the north by the rising shore of the mainland; the waters of the Gulf Stream flowing through these seas brought soft air and warmth and mild winters. Generations of sheep had made the soil of the Rough Island deeply fertile, and though where it confronted the mainland the shore was high and rocky, there were also many sweet slopes that leant towards a pale and sandy shore. There were small bays and sheltered crannies, a cave with a silver sanded floor, that Rob and Ella called *the dry cave*. Seals and sea-birds haunted those waters; there was always one call or another to be heard. The island was perhaps a quarter of a mile wide and less than twice as long. It made a small world but a huge garden. It had been Mr Alexander's declared intention to cultivate every yard of it, even where gorse tangled, even where the rock broke through the soil. That had been a long time ago.

'Tell of the day you met the Laird, Granda,' said Ella, time and again – in winter at the fireside, in summer as they sat on the cliff-top at the end of a long day. Her pleasure in hearing the tale was matched by his delight in telling it. It was, however, a tantalizing story, for it had as yet no true ending.

'It was away many hundred miles. It was in London, fearful city. But my father had gone there to seek his fortune and never found it, and now I was to seek mine.'

'How old were you?' Rob asked next.

'It was my tenth birthday, the day. I had but one shilling. And that my mother gave me as she sent me away.'

'Granda, Granda!' soft-hearted Ella would cry at this.

'Aye, she sent me from my home. There were the twelve of us bairns and our father scarce cold in his grave. There was little more in the house than that one shilling.'

'Go on,' said Rob, gruff.

'Where should I turn then, but to the city? I ran by the coaches and sprang to open the doors when they stopped and the travellers came tumbling like apples from a barrel.'

'And the cobbles hard under your feet,' Rob prompted.

'The cobbles hard, hard indeed. There was ever a scutter and scurry of lads about the coaches. The gentlemen flung pennies and we must all scramble in the dirt to grab at them. Then, also, there were the gentlemen's horses to be held outside great houses – at night, maybe, when the links flared to light the way. Or outside merchants' warehouses, where many went to buy wine or tobacco . . .'

One day there had been a young man in his twenties who had paused a second to look into the boy's scarecrow face. It was Mr Alexander, his tender conscience already sorely troubled. At times, when this tale was told, Ella and Rob were able to prompt their grandfather into great detail about this first meeting. Then he would recall even what Mr Alexander had been wearing – his caped greatcoat, his fine waistcoat, his fob watch and seals; and his steady expression; the firmness of his hand, not threatening but consoling; the weather, cold rain and a keen wind, the puddles, the hoofs striking sparks from the cobbles, the clamour of rumbling wheels, shouting men, barking dogs; the smell of London . . . At other times he kept to the point, which was that Mr Alexander had taken him home, the lad running at the horse's side, and handed him over to the housekeeper of a great gloomy city mansion. He became a part of the household, working in the kitchen, in the pantry, in the cellars. One day he had been watering the plants in the conservatory, and young Mr Alexander had come upon him and stood watching silently.

Then he said, 'John, I have a home far over the Border, in that land which bred us both. There I shall one day soon have all my being. I shall make a garden there. How if you come with me and help me with the task?'

'Aye, sir!' chorused Ella and Rob.

'Aye, sir,' echoed their grandfather. 'I will come.'

'Come once, stay ever,' Mr Alexander had said then. And 'Aye, sir,' the boy had answered yet again.

So they had made the long journey north, and come to the island. The house had been re-built and the garden made. Spit for spit, John Maitland said with pride, they worked together, though he was still not much more than a child. At twenty, John married Ellen, a girl from the mainland, and that same year Mr Alexander brought home a bride.

'The most beautiful of all the treasures in that house,' said Ella, prompting in her turn.

'Never doubt it. The young Mrs Alexander was the most beautiful of all the treasures in that house, Ella – bonny as an angel – and flown too soon. She died, poor lass, almost as soon as her son let out his first cry. Many's the night thereafter I'd watch Mr Alexander pacing the cliffs and crying after her – *Mary! Mary!* Crying and crying in his sore grief and bitter loneliness, knowing there was none could give him comfort – she would never come to him again!'

The words rolled out, the tears warmed Ella's eyes, but Rob went red with embarrassment. He hated this part of the story. He preferred the next bit, about how their grandmother, Ellen Maitland, took on the care of the baby, all the years until the day he was sent away to school; how he and Margaret, their own mother, had been playmates; how all the years the island was changing, growing in loveliness, flowering more profusely, constantly altered or added to, as Mr Alexander journeyed in search of plants and carried them home in triumph.

So the tale went on, with another man coming at last to work with them in the garden that had become so demanding. He was Wallace Ross, who married Margaret and fathered Ella and Rob ... Now that she was older, Ella had come to feel that Granda shook his head when he came to this point in the tale. But then he would make much of them both, as if he feared he might have suggested that it was a bad day when Margaret met Ross; for certainly if she had not, there would have been no Ella and no Rob ...

Each time this tale was told, both Ella and Rob hoped they might learn more. For they had never been told why Mr Alexander went away, why he had never returned, where he was now, what had become of his son. In the days that followed Wallace Ross's funeral, Ella's mind was filled with a further question, one which had entered it unbidden as she stood with her mother before Mrs Alexander's great wardrobe. It became so urgent that, cold with alarm at her own boldness, she was obliged to put it into words.

'What if Mr Alexander is dead, mother?'

Without bothering to look at her, her mother replied, 'You've no cause to fash yourself about what does not concern you.'

'I was just thinking –'

'Leave thinking to them that's wiser than you are.'

And that was the end of the matter.

But now Ella, made bold by her imaginings and by having once given the question words, repeated it to her grandfather.

'Granda – what if Mr Alexander has died? What if he never comes home to Innis Gharaidh?'

'You have death in your mind just now, lassie. Mr Alexander's no great age.'

He must be immensely old, Ella thought. Her grandfather spoke of himself as old, and she knew there was ten years at least between them. Hadn't Mr Alexander just come of age and inherited his fortune when first he met John Maitland, who was no more than a wee boy then? Mr Alexander must be going on for eighty years, which seemed as old to Ella as any prophet in the Bible. 'He does not send letters, Granda.'

'Word would come if he had died. And there would be an end to the money.'

Money for the upkeep of the island and those who lived and

worked there came regularly as clockwork from **Mr Alexander's**
Edinburgh bank. The family had never gone short, for there
was little enough to spend it on save seed that grew them food
as well as flowers, the occasional pig for salting down, or mutton
killed on the mainland and stored in the cold chamber under
the cottage floor. Sometimes they needed extra feed for the goats
that gave them milk, and there was sugar for the hives to be
thought of, and corn for the hens. Like the rest who lived in these
remote parts, they sent away for their clothes as they needed
them, taking what came and altering as necessary, getting cloth
in large bolts – so that for summer after summer Ella's cotton
dresses and her mother's were of the same colour and design. So
with the jerseys that kept them warm in winter – they were
the same for all the family, though Margaret did her best to
vary them by knitting different patterns. Such supplies came
by steamer from the railhead, down the loch and into the Sound.

'What if the money was not sent from the bank?' Ella insisted.

'Then indeed we would know we had lost our good friend.
That would be great sorrow – great sorrow.'

'What would become of us then, Granda?'

He did not answer her at once, but seemed to go right away
from her into his own thoughts. Ella knew she had put a
dreadful doubt into his mind by her nagging, and she wanted
nothing but to send it away.

'It will come! The money will come!' she cried. 'And Mr
Alexander – one day he'll be home!'

She hung lovingly on the old man's arm, intent on comforting him. But he shook her off, muttering to himself, 'He
could not. He could not ever take it from me ...' Then he roused
himself, and tweaking at her hair laughed at her foreboding
and said there was enough to keep them for many a day – she
was not to worry, but to trust him and her mother.

'She's been aye a thrifty soul, I thank the good Lord. We'll
no starve the long while ... But we'll starve if we bide talking
and not working! Ella – away now to the cabbages with your
hoe. Find Rob – he shall help you along the rows.'

Their father had been the one who first set them to work in

the garden. That had been three years ago, the very day after Miss Christabel called to see if they might come to school. Ella had been eleven years old and at that time a rather frail child; she had wept over the now familiar job that had seemed so hard and unending. 'It's labour not learning's your station in life,' her father had said grimly, with no thought of drying her tears. 'See you keep it and be content. You're never scholars, you and Rob, but only the gardener's grandchildren.'

She always remembered what he had called them – not his children, but the grandchildren of John Maitland, the gardener. She recalled now that their father, though he had worked in Mr Alexander's great garden like the rest of them, had been impatient of planting and pruning and the tenderness of seedlings, content to work the soil and mow the turf and live comfortably with his wife's family ...

That day, Ella worked without being aware of what she was doing, kicking aside the stones automatically, finding the late summer ground baked hard as rock. The doubts she had put into her grandfather's mind were her own doubts – about the future, about what might happen to them all, about other people coming to the island, living in Mr Alexander's house; about being sent away. Sent away – where? The island had been left in their grandfather's care. *Keep it as we both would wish until I return* ... That much she knew, and that it had happened just before she was born. John Maitland had kept his part of the bargain, but Mr Alexander had not returned. There must be something that happened next ...

The glade where Ella went next to work after hoeing down the cabbage rows with Rob, was hedged about with great bushes on which the roses had long passed and now the hips were brightening. The glade was open at one end, looking out over gently sloping ground that ran eventually to the shore. A path wound from the silvery sand of a magical small bay, rising gently and gracefully, until at last it reached the house, first passing the cottage and the outbuildings of Ella's own home.

As Ella came into the glade she looked down to the bay by long habit. There was a boat pulled up on the edge, and in the sand, faintly seen, a trail of footsteps. Someone was walking up the path. There was a slight, light sound of swishing against the bordering grasses.

Ella stood waiting. After a second or two, she saw Miss Christabel walking towards her, bareheaded in the sunshine.

They sat in the parlour, which was not much used. The window had been hastily opened, but the sill was littered with flies that had died trying to escape, and Margaret Ross had no opportunity to sweep them away.

'We have few visitors,' she said, fussed. 'The kettle's near boiling. You'll take a cup of tea?'

'Thank you. I will,' said Miss Christabel.

She must have been relieved, Ella thought, dead flies or no, that there was a better reception for her this time.

Miss Christabel smiled at Ella as her mother left the room.

'You live in Paradise,' she said. 'This island is Paradise.'

Ella did not know what to say. She gazed at Miss Christabel, surely the most beautiful person for miles around. Mrs Alexander had been beautiful, so they said, but she could not have matched Miss Christabel, Ella was certain. The visitor had put on her hat as she neared the house, but it by no means covered her hair, a reddish gold, very soft and lightly curling, yet with a shine to it, too. Her eyes were nearer a pale sea green than blue, and she had a clear skin that flushed over the cheekbones, lips pink rather than red. She was not very tall. She sat graceful and still, warm, sympathetic yet commanding. She came from a different part of the country and had had difficulty at first in getting along with the local people.

'I am here to ask again, shall you and your brother be let come to school. Do you wish to come, Ella?'

Ella nodded, still speechless.

'And your brother?'

Ella hesitated, bit her lip, sadly shook her head.

'You both can read and write, I daresay?'

'Aye,' said Ella in a small voice, responding to some anxiety in Miss Christabel. 'Granda learnt us.'

'Your grandfather is a fine man.'

'Aye,' said Ella again, but this time smiling.

'What besides has he taught you?'

'Sums. Kings. About the world.'

'Why, that seems the most anyone might hope to learn! Have you books, then?'

'They are from Mr Alexander's house. Granda knew he'd not be minding the loan. But they have paper covers put to them – there is little damage.'

Miss Christabel laughed a little, but kindly and sympathetically.

'There'd be more damage – and to you children – were they not in your hands ... But, Ella – you should be at school. It is the law says so. I am surprised this was never told to your parents by the last schoolmaster.'

'He was aye drunk!' cried Ella. 'They'd all play truant and he never knew a name of any one. Any'll tell you that was a grand easy time at the school!'

Miss Christabel flushed, as she had done on her first visit to the house. 'Well, I must speak to your mother. Though I think she must know fine that every child shall go to school till fourteen years old.'

Ella did not reply. A cold disappointment took her voice away. She would be fourteen next birthday. It was therefore already too late. Only Rob, who did not want to, might get to school. If only the drunken dominie had seen himself off to his grave a year or two earlier so that Miss Christabel could come to the rescue sooner!

'I'd hope we might all be friends,' Miss Christabel said. 'What would you say?'

Ella did not have to answer this, for her mother came in with the tea tray. She had chivvied Rob indoors and now thrust him ahead of her.

'Here is my son, Robert, Miss Christabel. I call you *Miss Christabel*. It's a wee bit forward, maybe? Should I not rather call you *Miss Galbraith*?'

'I like fine to be called by my first name, Mrs Ross. It is

easy for the pupils in school and more friendly altogether. How do you do, Robert?'

'When I was at school,' Mrs Ross said, 'the master was none so friendly, I can tell you! Times have changed!'

'And for the better, so I believe.'

'Maybe so, maybe not. Will you be taking milk and sugar?'

'No sugar, thank you.'

Thus politely they handed the little sentences back and fore across the teacups, advancing and withdrawing like figures in some formal ritual. They spoke of the weather, of the fishing, of the harvest, of Lizzie Best, whom Miss Christabel knew as Mistress Maclean. Mrs Ross remarked that Miss Christabel had not been home these summer holidays, and Miss Christabel replied that since her father had died and her sister married there was now no family home.

'You've just the one sister?'

'I have.'

'That is hard for you. But you will be leaving us yourself to get wed very soon, no doubt.'

Miss Christabel smiled. 'I have plenty to do just now. And I am sure you know what I wish to ask you this day, Mrs Ross. I am hoping you are of a different way of thinking – different from your late husband's ... Shall the children come soon to school? Did you know they must do so – it is the law.'

Ella and Rob both stared at their mother, but with very different expressions – hers eager, his scowling and anxious.

'I have not yet thought of the matter,' Margaret replied. 'It's the journey across makes it hard. It is not always calm weather as it is today. Both can handle a boat fairly – but not in rough water ... We shall have to see.' This time she smiled at the visitor. 'Ella's a big girl to start schooling. Have you others as old?'

'I have two girls and a boy. The rest go to work this year, I am sad to say.'

'They are country children. They are needed. What father is it lets his son stay so late at school?'

'No father at all, Mistress Macmillan of Glentorra. Hamish

Macmillan is a clever boy. It would be a sin should he be stopped in his schooling,' Miss Christabel said, warming, flushing a little, her voice undoubtedly sharpening. 'He may well gain a scholarship. We'll see him away to St Andrews yet!'

Mrs Ross smiled and tutted. 'What ideas are they that you put into his head – he's a widow's only son.' But Ella's heart leapt at these words, so unlike any she had ever heard, so full of bravery and challenge and promise. Hamish Macmillan was the big boy whose nose Rob had punched in Lizzie Best's parlour after the funeral.

'Please, mother,' Ella said, clearing her throat yet still producing no more than a whisper. 'If it was rough weather could we not stop overnight with the Macleans?'

'Whisht, Ella – mind your tongue and let things be that you've not the means to understand ... I'll think of the matter, Miss Christabel. May I give you some more tea?'

Miss Christabel went slowly away down the path that wound to the shore, and Ella went with her. She thought her mother had called her back, but she chose not to hear. It was a sunny day but not too hot. The garden was moving towards its decline and in the next many weeks there would be a great deal of work to do. For Ella and for Rob the days would be long and hard.

'I doubt there'll be time for school,' Ella said, half to herself, yet hoping Miss Christabel might hear and answer – as indeed she did.

'There's always time to learn, Ella,' she said, stopping in her tracks and turning, speaking very earnestly and keenly, sounding positive and encouraging. 'What if I should lend you books? I could do that. Teach yourself what you can. In the winter evenings, now, when you sit quiet by the hearth – was not this when your grandfather taught you?'

Ella nodded. 'Oh, I'd like fine you should loan me the books!' she cried. 'Oh indeed, I would! I would!'

'Then that's settled. When any of you come to the mainland, I shall see there's a parcel left with Maggie at the post. But tell your mother at once. We want no secrets.'

On the shore the tide had lifted the boat and it tugged eagerly at the ring in the rock to which it was tied. Ella ran into the water and pulled the boat round, afraid that Miss Christabel might dabble the hem of her skirt in the salt sea. The sea was smooth, a little breeze merely ruffling it far out beyond the headland, beyond the reef where the puffins paused when they made their sudden trips from out beyond the lighthouse. Now the reef had vanished under the incoming tide and a few gulls screamed as if they had lost for ever what they most desired. Later, when the tide ran full, the gannets would come to plunge and soar and beat the air and cleave the water with their strong wings and terrible beaks.

'Good-bye! Good-bye!' cried Miss Christabel, as she rowed away with her hat in the bottom of the boat and her hair lifting and blowing about her face.

Ella stood waving. Her heart was full of excitement and hopeful possibility. Surely she had been right to think that everything would be different now? Yet she knew that her grandfather would not release her from her usual tasks, nor Rob from his – he had never protested when their father set them to work. Two extra pairs of hands, even such small ones, had been welcome. By now those hands were stronger and worked with some knowledge and confidence. Ella knew what Rob had not yet understood and she would not willingly tell him – she knew that deeply and fondly as their grandfather cared for them, he cared even more for the garden, and to the garden he would most surely sacrifice any and everything, even his loved grandchildren.

When she came up from the shore, Ella did not return to the glade. Miss Christabel was by now round the headland, so there was no use looking for the boat from there. She left her work and ran on, eventually crossing the lawn before the house, taking the short cut through the orchard, set within its protecting wall, and out through the gate on the far side, along the track between the rhododendrons, and those azaleas whose

29

leaves were now just tinted with a hint of autumn. Beyond them the heather was like bright waves, like a coloured waterfall, caught into stillness as it tumbled down the cliff side.

Ella came out on the far side of the heather, where the cliff began once more to subside, and there below her was the anchorage they most often used, with a stone jetty to protect their boats against harsh weather. It was a harbour on which Mr Alexander and her grandfather had laboured together, the year after Mrs Alexander died . . .

Far out, almost to the other shore, Ella saw Miss Christabel's boat, making such good time on the ingoing tide that it would soon beach safely. Watching her, Ella suddenly widened her nostrils at the smell of pipe smoke. John Maitland, the only man on the island, did not touch tobacco. Ella stepped forward until she was looking directly down the cliff and the hanging heathers.

Immediately below her, a man was sitting on the rocks. His boat was tied up, and he lounged easily on his perch, as if a frequent and familiar visitor to the place.

The sun was behind Ella. As she stood on the cliff edge, her shadow was flung across the sand below and across the frilled edge of the water, which strangely distorted it. She saw too late that the shadow laid itself across the stranger's feet, and before she could step back he saw the shadow and turned to look upwards. He rose, and they stood gazing at one another – he dwarfed by the drop and the distance, she made into a giant by the declining sun's projection of her long shadow.

The man was George Erskine, whom her mother had said might be willing to come and work for them on the island. As Ella recognized him, she turned away quickly, pulling her shadow after her. Then, on the far path that went down in steps to the island harbour, she saw her mother slowly descending, her back straight, her head high, a light shawl over her hair.

3

In November Ella was fourteen. The day after her birthday she was running fast down the path to the beach, carrying, in a neat parcel, two of the books that Miss Christabel had lent her.

'Wait!' she called. Then shouted it angrily. 'Wait! Bide till I come!'

The man at the oars held the boat steady, looking up at Ella. She began to slither in her haste. For two days the rain had barely ceased and the ground here was like oil. She would end flat on her back unless she took care. She reached the shore at last and ran across to the boat, breathless and anxious, calling out again in that furious voice –

'You're to take the books! Take the books with you!'

Now that the rain was past there was a great stillness over everything. The grey sea barely stirred, the grey horizon melted and merged. As sights blurred, sounds became magnified. Ella could hear gulls screaming out of sight over a mackerel shoal, and maybe they could hear her.

'*Wait!*' shouted Ella.

'I am waiting,' he answered quietly, still holding the boat just out of her reach. 'Need you be screeching after me like a stormcock?'

'I feared you'd leave without the books.'

'Maybe I will, too.' He gave her a long cold look and said clearly, 'Am I to take my orders from you, brat that you are?'

Ella's hands began to shake and she was filled with a kind of furious terror. She scowled at him across the few feet of water, helpless until he helped her, knowing he might torment her by withholding that help. He was none but George Erskine, a man from the far side of the country, hired to help her grandfather in the garden, and so, she felt, she might order him if she chose. But she knew, as Rob knew, too, that he was something more. Though he was in colour and features totally different yet, in some curious way, he reminded both Ella and Rob of their father. Something in his manner, in his height and weight, in his outline, made him seem an echo, a shadow of familiar memories. Perhaps that was why their mother behaved to him so easily. He had only been a few months in the neighbourhood, yet her manner seemed to suggest that she had known him a long time.

'Well,' he said now, 'I'll be away to my lodgings.'

'The books! There'll be a parcel waiting. They'll be with Maggie. At the post.'

'I'll maybe not pass that way.'

She did not answer, but stood fighting the tears that were not so much in her eyes as in her throat.

'Say *Please*, and I could be thinking better of it.'

He would not have spoken to her like this if her mother or her grandfather had been near; yet she knew she would not be able to complain to them.

'Please,' she said, loathing herself.

'That's fine, then,' he said. He manoeuvred the boat so that the keel just touched on the shingle. He reached out for the parcel – then held it poised above the water. 'What comes next?'

'Don't drop them!' she squealed, to save herself answering. But she was bound to, for the sake of the books that were Miss Christabel's. 'Thank you,' she said, between her teeth.

He nodded, laid the parcel down on his rolled jacket, for he was rowing in his shirt sleeves as if it were no more than a day in earliest autumn, and pulled away fast.

Ella turned back at once up the cliff path, bitterly smearing her hand across her eyes. The heather that had been so fine and flowery was rusted with the end of the year. Half of it had been clipped back and was tidy, but the rest was yet to be done. It was a back-breaking and often giddy job, for it was frequently necessary to balance right out over the drop. Even their father had never let the children do this job, but as George Erskine had said, it was better for someone small and light and agile, than for a heavy man like himself, or an older one inclined to sudden breathlessness. Ever since Erskine had come to the island to help John Maitland with the great weight of work, Ella and Rob had found themselves doing much more. It seemed to make little sense. As for going to school, the matter had not been spoken of since the day Miss Christabel came calling.

Ella found Rob at the head of the path.

'I heard what he said to you. Will I hole his boat the morrow? Will I, Ella?'

'Yon's Tam Dougal's boat – he's none of his own.'

He more than half meant it, and that seemed to stretch out the year between them, for she would not even have used such words, let alone put them into practice. Again she felt vaguely frightened, knowing that Rob was still a child, that she had suddenly become twice as wise and must depend on herself for both their sakes – though she could not imagine at present what this might mean.

'Come away in,' she said. He looked a scarecrow in the old torn jersey that he wore for working in the garden, his trousers cut short from a pair of his father's and rolled up high. He was barefoot, and his knees were red under an earthy covering that came from shuffling along the paths between the rose beds, giving them their last strict weeding of the season. 'You've a chilblain come to your little toe,' she said, rather sharply, as if she blamed him for it. He looked a very small boy to her in her new wisdom, and since she knew he would not take comfort she was bound to scold instead.

He muttered something and stumped away from her, anxious to be indoors. And it was good to go inside. There was the

33

cat purring, the peaty smell from the hearth, their mother with the kettle in one hand and the old brown pot in the other.

'Just in time,' she said. 'Wash your hands, both, and come to the table. Your grandfather needs his tea.'

Rob and Ella had never spoken together of George Erskine until after the day Rob suggested damaging his boat. Certainly it had been necessary to get more help now that their father was gone. At that season of the year, as it would have been in the spring, they had needed to replace the lost pair of hands. There had been no other man on the mainland in want of work as the harvest ended – only George Erskine, the stranger in the community, had been free.

'What will he know of gardens, Margaret?' the old man had said.

'What you teach him, father – and that's like to be plenty. I'll thank you not to kill yourself overworking. I cannot do without you – nor can the children. They look to you now.'

In fact they had 'looked to' him ever since they could remember. But even if Rob did not entirely take in what their mother had said, Ella understood. Ella wanted their grandfather to live for ever and perhaps had never paused to consider that such things do not happen; he must die like anyone else. The fear that he might make himself ill by working too hard – that he might work himself to death, as it is said – had almost made her join in the conversation – only she knew her mother would tell her to hold her tongue. She stayed silent, but the threat had stayed in her mind and because of it she had endured the arrival, the continued presence of George Erskine.

'Will I tell the name I have for him?' Rob asked, almost under his breath.

They were sitting together in a private chink in the cliffside which, even in winter days, caught all possible sunshine.

'Tell me.'

'It is *Sgarbh*.'

Ella bit her lip, half shocked, half excited. The word meant *cormorant*, and it was a good name, ugly and black. Just as a

34

cormorant would sit for lengths of time on a rock, staring none knew where, so George Erskine had stood on the cliff top as they rowed home from their father's funeral. That was the first time they had become properly aware of him, though he had come once to the island in search of work when there was none to offer. He did also give an impression of blackness, as a cormorant does, having very dark hair and a thick moustache that drooped either side of his mouth, hiding much of his expression.

'Do you find the name good?' asked Rob.

'I do.'

Rob settled himself into the hollow, digging into it with his bottom and shoulders, as if he would like to be a part of the cliff itself. He spoke again in that hushed voice.

'I fear him.'

Ella did not answer, and after a bit he nudged her and repeated, 'I fear him. Do you fear him, Ella?'

She said again, 'I do.'

'Why?'

But this she would not tell him, though she knew why. She had put it into thoughts, but not words. In her heart, in the very back of her mind was this terrible thought: that her mother liked him very well, that widows did marry again – as Lizzie Best had married Donald Maclean – and that one day they might find themselves, not merely with a new father, but with George Erskine. Their mother was not so old. She was certain to be lonely. One day, however much Ella might not care to think of it, their grandfather would no longer be with them. Who would care for them then? Their mother would think of all this, of the future and what it might hold, of their strange insecurity on the island where nothing was, in fact, their own. There was every need for her to marry again – and who, Ella wondered, thinking around the men on the mainland, was the right age and free? She knew none of them well, but she knew them by sight and name. One of the games she and Rob liked to play was to sit staring across to the village, picking out the houses, naming those who lived in them, imagining what they might be doing at that moment, and envying them their dogs, for they

35

had never been allowed one of their own. In all those comfortable crofts there was no man Ella could choose for her mother to marry. They were either family men already or they were young lads courting. There was no one but George Erskine.

'Why do you fear him?' Rob insisted. There was something like tears in his voice, he sounded choked. He said, as if he had read her thoughts, 'Aye – I know why! I know fine!'

'You cannot.'

'I do, so.'

'Say it.'

'No! No – I will not say it, Ella!'

She was silent. He huddled against her and she would have liked to comfort him and herself by putting her arm round him. If she did, he would give in and cry, so she stayed still and stiff, staring out to sea. It was high tide. There was not a bird in sight. But quiet and gentle somewhere below them, the eider drifted round the headland, from sheltered bay to sheltered bay, croodling modestly but insistently as they went. Ella thought how Sgarbh had tormented her last night, first seeming to row away, then holding Miss Christabel's books over the water as if he meant to drop them in ... Yet this morning he had come with a fresh supply that Miss Christabel had left for her, and had smiled as he handed them to her. Perhaps it was unfair, just an indulging of her suspicions, to remember that her mother had been there at the time.

'He's maybe one to improve on acquaintance,' she said.

It was a sentiment often expressed by Lizzie Best, but Rob only said, 'I'm not wanting to know him better.'

He shifted away from her slightly, as if pulling himself together. He muttered something quickly under his breath, glanced at Ella sharply to see if she had heard, and turned very red. Ella heard what he said. She flushed in her turn, saying, 'Whisht, away with you!' as her mother might.

He had said: '*They'll get wed.*'

There was a long silence between them, but Rob's thought must have continued, and had carried him far before he spoke again.

36

'I'll maybe marry myself when I'm grown,' he said.

'Who'd marry you?'

'I might tell –'

'Go on then, you daft thing – I dare you!'

'I'll marry Miss Christabel.'

'You will not! You'd never be old enough!'

That made them both laugh, and after a while they felt easier and came out of hiding. Their grandfather, who had been all day among the roses, was picking up his fork, then slipping his pruning knife into his pocket. The day's work was over and since tomorrow was Sunday they could look forward to a little rest and a good dinner – a jiggot of mutton, maybe, and stoved potatoes. Sunday was a stern day, however, with little fun to it; Ella and Rob wished often and often that some other day in the week could be the day of rest ... Still, after the dinner there would be Miss Christabel's books – she often marvelled she was let read anything so giddy on the Sabbath. Once Granda had seemed doubtful about it but her mother had overruled him.

Some of these books were lesson books, no doubt slipped in by Miss Christabel as a pill for the rest of the jam. But there were also fat books telling tales of bravery and adventure, that Rob liked Ella to read aloud; and others full of heroes and warriors and beautiful maidens, of youngest sons winning fortunes and wooing the daughters of kings ...

The whole world had been changed for Ella by these tales, the very clouds were coloured. She looked at the three or four volumes lent at a time, and she imagined all the other books in all the world that waited to be opened. She read much to Rob, and, agreeably enough, she read aloud in the evenings to her mother and to Granda – as in fact she had done ever since she had been taught by him to read. In those days there had been only a handful of story books taken from the shelves in the house. Some of these books had belonged to the Laird's young son, William. They were mostly bold adventuring tales of a sort Rob quite liked – but Miss Christabel's books were much better. They carried Ella into a land peopled with paragons, where toil and distress faded to the contented promise of ever after. It was not reading them aloud that she most enjoyed, but being secret with them, hunched in a corner, fingers in her ears against the common clatter of daily conversation. And when she went to bed she lay long half awake, imagining herself into a thousand magical situations, insinuating herself among the high-born and the beautiful, whose trials and disasters would be nobly resolved, virtue triumphant, love guiding all ... Miss Christabel seemed to have unending supplies of this enchantment – but even should the books run out, Ella would be happy to start again at the beginning and read through to the last page of the last book, never missing a syllable. And except for the delights of being taught every day by Miss Christabel, Ella was certain that what she now enjoyed was better than any school had ever been or could ever be. She worked in the garden a bit slower every day, her thoughts were so busy – but so far Granda seemed not to have noticed.

'There'll be storms,' Margaret Ross said, looking from the cottage door, out, out across the Sound and on into the stretches of the great ocean. 'It's true winter soon, father.'

He looked where she looked, looked around him, sniffed the air. 'The winter will be mild, forebye,' he said.

'But rough.'

'Aye. Maybe rough. Now and then.'

'We'll need to re-stake the saplings beyond the house this week.'

'The man's about it.'

'And the small greenhouse – I notice a pane of glass gone. Have we glass, father?'

'We have. Cut and ready.' His mouth twitched as he looked at her, for she knew much and never stinted advice, but she confined her energies to the house and would only consent to gather the vegetables and cut a flower or two; no doubt she was wise. 'Ah, Margaret,' he said, 'setting us all to work again, I see!'

'And there's the espalier along the south wall looks a wee bit poorly. Should it not be cut back hard this year? And the medlar – I was looking at the medlar.' She broke off as she saw him smiling into his beard. 'I have my sight, father, and my wits about me! Did you note the walnut? There was some scorch on the leaves after the last gale. I doubt it's a tree for these parts.'

'The walnut is thirty year and more growing. It was planted by Mr Alexander and it stands forty feet. Is not that enough?'

'There was a poor crop the year.'

'There are bad years and good years for all.'

'It had better have been a spruce he planted just there,' Margaret insisted. 'Take down the walnut now and it'll fetch a good price.'

'You are full of wisdom, lass,' he said. 'But you know fine I'll not take down a tree Mr Alexander planted – not one that's healthy. Next year's crop will be better.'

'Walnut is a wood much sought,' she insisted. 'We could do with some money of our own.'

'How would it be our own? We had as likely call the furniture in his house our own.'

' "Take what you need," he said.'

' "Keep all as I would wish," he said also.'

Margaret turned away, went into the kitchen and clattered the dishes in the sink.

'Rob needs boots,' she said, when her father followed her, 'I must have wool for winter knitting.'

'When the money comes, you shall have what's needed.'

'It is two weeks after time. Dry the dishes,' she said sharply to Ella, who had been making herself small.

'And then find Rob for me, Ella,' her grandfather said. 'I need the paving round the house sweeping – there's a great fall of dead leaves still lying. Find him and tell him – then come to me in the big greenhouse.'

He went out and they could see him crossing beyond the cottage towards the greenhouses, walking rather slowly.

'Will I polish the spoons?' asked Ella.

'I spoke hardly to him,' her mother muttered. 'I should remember he's not so young as he was ... Get away to him, Ella, and help all you can.'

All that morning, Ella worked with her grandfather in the greenhouse. He did not speak much, except to instruct her. Far away, through the gate in the small walled garden where more delicate plants grew, Ella could see Rob sweeping the dead leaves. As fast as he drew them into a pile the wind whisked them away from him, drawing them upwards, spinning them into a neat pretty spiral, then dropping them again just out of his broom's reach. She watched how he kept his temper through this teasing and knew that if she had been at the task she would have been shouting angrily by now, flinging down the broom, stamping away ... Though he was younger than she was, Rob was in some ways stronger, and Ella knew this. She would always be cleverer, but Rob would be the stronger, not just in his body and muscles, but in his nature; his anger did not flare like hers, it was steady and lasted long.

There was much to be done in the greenhouse. It was a time for clearing and cleaning. The glass must be washed down, the shelves scoured, the gravel in the pans on the staging run through clean water. Great piles of flower pots, stacked according to size, fitted neatly into one another, up and up into a kind of chimney, must be cleaned and disinfected for the new plants they would receive. The tasks seemed endless. In the corners, spiders and other creatures had tucked away hopefully for the winter, but they had all to be brushed out. This greenhouse was the garden's heart, therefore the heart of the island, for it was full of beginnings. Ella sometimes thought her grandfather said most of his prayers in the greenhouse, for he often stood muttering over a plant, or with his lips just moving bowed his head as if asking for help with some fractious or ailing treasure.

As they worked through the morning together, speaking very little, the wind increased and the sea grew high and agitated. A huge flight of gulls flew inland on the wind, that lifted and hurled them, so that they swooped and turned, cutting the air with the sharp blades of their wings. The grey sky increased their whiteness, their black heads or backs or wing tips looked like splashes of pitch.

The old man stooped to lift a wooden box full of odd sized pots that must be graded. It was big and heavy. Lifting it on to the shelf, he set it short, caught the edge. The box fell from his hands, crashing to the ground. Pots cascaded and shattered.

Ella cried out and ran to help. But it was more than just an accident or a misjudgement.

'Granda? Granda, are you well?'

He was leaning over the staging, breathing very deep and hard, and she seemed to feel the breath tearing at him as he dragged it up out of his lungs – making it, Ella thought, making breath like a spider making web . . .

'I'll fetch Mother . . .'

'No!' he said, gasping but sharp.

'You're ill!' she cried, not knowing how shrill and afraid she sounded.

'I'm a wee bit short of breath, lassie,' he answered, already recovering. 'I'll thank you to hold your tongue about the matter.'

Ella thought how she and Rob had talked of George Erskine, of Sgarbh, and longed for him to be gone. Now she saw how necessary it was for her grandfather to have another man about the place, and knew that for his sake they must somehow contain their dislike of the newcomer. They could hope to take care of Granda only in this way, a way that seemed so very disagreeable.

From the cottage came the sound of a spoon beaten on a tin plate.

'It's dinner time, Granda.'

'Now do as I bid you, Ella Ross – keep that tongue silent in your head, I trust you, mind.'

She nodded. They went out of the greenhouse, the door carefully closed behind them.

'We'll be half done in there by dusk,' he said. He paused a second, looking down at her. He put out his hand and

41

pinched her cheek gently, smiling over his beard. 'You've lost your colour, foolish lass. A man grows older – and the pieces of him wear a little thin. Grass and the flower of grass ... Do you understand?'

'... withered and fallen away,' she murmured, looking at the ground.

'Come away in, now,' he said, taking her hand.

Mother was waiting by the stove, the cat rubbing sly and hopeful round her skirts, and Rob was already indoors, blowing on his chilled fingers; George Erskine was washing his hands under the scullery pump. When they were all settled, Granda said grace. Ella squeezed her eyelids together, but however hard she tried, they sprang open. She was sure her mother and Sgarbh would be looking at one another across the table, secretly smiling. But she was wrong. Margaret's eyes were closed, while Sgarbh had clasped his hands together and meekly bowed his head ...

'Amen,' they all said, and Margaret ladled the broth.

'The storm'll be worse before it's better,' she said. 'There'll be little chance of rowing to the mainland the day.'

Ella looked quickly at Rob, and then they both paid attention to their bowls. Sgarbh would be bound to stay on the island. Most storms took at least three days to blow themselves out.

4

'There is something different,' John Maitland said, holding the letter in his hand, frowning a little.

Every quarter day since Mr Alexander had left the island, the letter that accompanied the money sent from his Edinburgh bank had been in precisely the same words: 'Herewith, on the instruction of our client, William Hamilton Alexander Esq ...' Then the amount in figures and written words and a polite request that the enclosed receipt be signed and posted. Four times in each of the mounting years this letter had come to the island with utter reliability and regularity. This quarter it was three weeks overdue and when it was opened there was a change: 'Herewith, on the instructions of our client, please find the sum ...' And so on.

'He is not named,' said John. 'Why is that?'

'It's maybe a new clerk wrote the letter, father.' Margaret laughed a little, hoping to rally her father, and satisfied that the money had come, never mind the rest. The other'd be an old man by now. He'll have given up work – or maybe been promoted. How's that?'

'There's some change – and it's no in the handwriting.'

'Och, father, away with you! You know fine we'd hear if he died.'

'If he left in his will that the money should still be paid ...'

'It could never be without we heard of it. His lawyer would write. Or his heirs. He will have heirs with such a fortune. Heirs to the money – to the island. We could well be sent away from here.'

43

Ella was sitting hunched in the chimney corner, trying to shut her ears and get on with her reading. But the tone of the voices, the pattern of the conversation had come between her and the tale of Sir Gawaine. She pretended to read but in spite of herself she felt her ears stretch wide. Where would we go? Where? Who would it be who sent us? When her mother spoke of *heirs* Ella seemed to see them as some tramping army, a force come to occupy the island, to hurl its inhabitants from the rocks into the sea . . .

Then, when her mother did not speak again, Ella looked up. Her mother had turned away to deal with some household matter, but her grandfather stood by the window, looking out over the island that he had made so much a garden that barely a square yard remained uncultivated.

Up by the house stretched lawns sheltered by carefully grouped shrubs – azaleas, rhododendrons. The house in its turn was a shelter for the early flowering camellias that must be placed so that the sun never fell on their frosted petals. In spring, sweeping away from the edges of the grass, huge drifts of snowdrops and crocuses, of daffodils and narcissi of all kinds, frothed and gleamed beneath bare branches, stretching away to the far cliff tops, where primroses were scattered as freely as confetti. Besides all this, each outcrop of rock, each break and pocket in the cliffs was a garden on its own, holding plants cunningly planned by John Maitland's long experience each for its environment – some where the bare rock face caught the sun and afforded the heat they needed, others where a spring trickled to supply the moisture that they loved; and always some shelter cleverly contrived for such as would not stand salt winds.

'I had best write to the bank, Margaret,' John Maitland said, turning from the window.

He fetched his pen and the bottle of blue ink, and some paper carefully spread on a blotter, as if to set about the task immediately. But after he had put the name of the island and the day's date, and written carefully in fine copper-plate, *Dear Sir*, he paused. He thrust the letter away from him.

44

'I cannot,' he said. 'It must be another day.'

'Aye,' said Margaret. 'Another day is soon enough.'

Ella tried to return to Sir Gawaine, but the story now seemed thin and unreal. Granda had left the kitchen. Her mother had spread the ironing blanket on the table, and the irons were heating on the stove, one big, one small.

'Where would we go?' asked Ella.

Her mother said 'Whisht!' as usual. But then she paused in her work, holding the iron in her hand, looking thoughtfully at Ella. 'You're no such a child now, Ella. I should answer you – and I would answer you. But I cannot tell you what I do not know.' She frowned, but then she smiled at Ella, saying she should not worry. There was nothing yet to be worried about.

It did not seem like that at all to Ella, and she insisted, 'But is he dead? Is Mr Alexander dead?'

'I know no more of that than you do. I have said so.'

'Then the island would belong to his son, mother.'

'Maybe.'

'I know how you played together when you were bairns – his mother being dead. He would not send you from your home. He would not – would he?'

Margaret hesitated. Then she said. 'He died. Mr Alexander's son died.'

This was totally new to Ella, she had to begin all over again with her fears and imaginings.

'You never said that before. Nor Granda.'

'There was an accident ... I find it hard to explain. I had sooner not speak of this, Ella. There was an accident. Let that be all for now. Another day. I'll maybe tell you more another day.'

Ella could not be silent, for her thoughts nibbled and nagged at the problem.

'If Mr Alexander's son is long dead, mother, then who shall have his fortune and the house and the island?'

'Now, Ella, get the matter out of your mind. Mr Alexander could well have married a second time. He was not anything near an old man when he went away.' She seemed to hesitate a second, then she said, 'People often marry for a second time.

Then, who knows, he may have other children in the world by now.'

Ella did not like any of this. She would far rather doom Mr Alexander to perpetual mourning for his beautiful lost wife – that was one thing. But the other was the way her mother had said that people often marry for a second time. It was as if she had slipped the words into a space found ready-made for them, taking advantage of an unhoped-for opportunity. Mr Alexander, at this, slid away from Ella's thought, and her whole mind became taken up with the more urgent problem. She longed to say, 'Would you? Mother – would you marry again?' but she had not the courage. She watched her mother fussing with the iron, which had grown cool while she talked, putting it back to heat and taking up the second one – and that was too hot.

'Don't stand there staring, Ella Ross,' said Margaret sharply. 'Take and fold the shirts – they're aired by now.'

Ella did as she was bid, turning to the clothes-horse standing round the fire. There were three shirts airing – one was Granda's, one was Rob's; the third belonged to Sgarbh. Ella left it until last.

Since the storm a week or two ago, when he had been honestly prevented from returning home, George Erskine had remained on the island. That first night, when the sea beat in up the Sound, the waves riding in like row upon row of horsemen, he had said he could easily reach the mainland. It was just a silly boast; only a magic boat, such as Ella might find in Miss Christabel's story books, could have survived in such boiling waters. He was given the loft over the stable, where there was straw in plenty to make a comfortable bed.

After two days the storm blew itself out, and in calm weather Sgarbh took himself to the mainland. He was away all that day and the next, and because he had worked, while he was living with them, at tasks not ordinarily his, he was missed. He was a very strong man, as the children's father had been until he became sick. In the days of storm he had put much in order that had lain waiting since Wallace Ross died. The old shed was tidied and a whole tree that had fallen one day last winter, was lopped of its branches and sawn into logs. Fierce as the wind blew in those days, he went down to the shore and harvested great piles of seaweed that had been flung up on to the rocks and would be swept away again unless it were claimed – John Maitland made seaweed into manure by a long process he said was his own and no other man's. Also, Sgarbh drew all the water in those days, and would not so much as let the others out of doors while the gale was so fierce. He milked the goat, collected the eggs, fed the fowl; only the geese seemed to resent him.

'There's many a man,' said Sgarbh, when John protested at being persuaded to stay indoors, 'took too little care and ended his days before his time.'

Ella looked quickly at her grandfather, expecting him to put Sgarbh in his place, to make some blistering retort and go stolidly about his own concerns. But he stayed silent. Perhaps he was remembering, as she was, how he had lifted the box of pots and the pain in his chest had snatched away his breath – as the wind might, should he step outside.

Later, Rob spoke to Ella in wonder of their grandfather's meekness.

'Sgarbh spoke good sense,' said Ella shortly.

'He'll no speak good sense to me!' boasted Rob.

Yet, when he had gone to the mainland, and stayed there one whole day and then the next, there came an uneasy feeling over the household that he might not return. Only Rob could rejoice in this, for Ella knew now how much her grandfather needed the man. She was torn between this need and the needs of her mother. Maybe Margaret must be considered, too. Certainly she was more lively when he was there, for during his absence she seemed hardly to speak, to be so deeply wrapped in her thoughts as hardly to be herself at all ... Besides, the storm had done a great deal of garden damage, and they were all at work as long as the light lasted, tying and lopping and sweeping. It was a hard moment to find themselves deprived of help.

On the third morning, a fine and smiling day, soft as September, laid itself along the coast as if no tumult had ever come out of those western waters to batter and destroy. The

47

gulls rocked on the water, and though the eider were not heard, for they had moved to better shelter before the storm began and had not yet returned, many other birds were about. Cormorant and shag flew in twos and threes over the face of the Sound, coming at last to some rock perch where they would stand, beaks up, to dry their plumage and stare. Far down the Sound, well out of sight, oyster catchers were busy picking and crying excitedly over the treasure the storm had tossed them.

When Ella straightened up from her task of clearing away blown twigs and small branches, she saw Sgarbh rowing towards the island. She called to Rob, and they stood together watching. The man in the boat saw them – or they thought he must see them – and as if against their wills, heavily yet in some way compelled, they waved.

'Why did you?' cried Rob, turning away.

'Why did *you*?'

He could not answer.

'Robbie,' said Ella, 'I think best we give over greeting for Granda's sake.'

'Oh aye,' he said at last, his voice wobbling. 'Aye. I see it also. But I wish I didna.'

'Run tell Mam he's back.' Seeing him hesitate, she grabbed his hand, and ran with him to the cottage.

'He's back,' said Rob to Margaret.

Their mother went slowly to the door and stood on the step, drying her hands on her apron.

'Set another place, Ella,' was all she said.

They felt half disappointed at her calm.

Half an hour later, George Erskine reached the cottage. He was dressed in his best suit, in spite of having rowed the two miles.

'We are glad to see you back,' Margaret said, but with no more than courtesy.

'Mistress Ross,' he said, 'I am come to say good-bye.'

Then truly Margaret stirred, though only in the sharp closing of her fingers, and in the way she lifted her head.

'Is it so?' she said.

'It is. They tell me my room is needed – there's a son come home from Australia or such parts. So I have my belongings with me in the boat – not that they're so many.'

At this moment the gardener came up to the cottage from the walled garden and paused on the threshold.

'Father,' said Margaret. 'George Erskine is come to bid good-bye. He has lost his lodging on the mainland.'

There was a pause that seemed a long one.

'Where shall he find other?' John Maitland said at last.

'There's none,' George Erskine answered. 'I'm away inland or down the coast. A sad time of year to be seeking work.'

'What would you say, father?' Margaret asked in a flat tone, as if she had no wish to influence him.

Again there was a pause. The old man knew that much was in the balance, but perhaps he did not care to name the ingredients.

'Did the loft let rain, when the storm was on it?' he asked Sgarbh.

'It did not.'

'Then it shall stand winter – should you not be too proud, forebye.'

'Thank you, Mr Maitland,' said Sgarbh.

'Fetch your things, man.'

'Thank you,' said Sgarbh again. 'I will do that.'

Of the four who watched him go, no one of them turned to any other. They kept their eyes and their thoughts to themselves. They went indoors silently, and sat silently at table. They waited for Sgarbh to return. Then John Maitland said Grace, and Margaret dished the stew, as if it were any other day. There was little conversation and the meal was soon done. Then they scattered to their work, only Margaret called Ella back.

'Come and help me. We have to find blankets for the loft.'

'He has some from last time,' said Ella.

'We shall try to make it more homely for him, since he's to stay.'

The loft was full of the fine smell of straw, of the chaff of many years. Each harvest they brought a load from the main-

49

land and stored it here, using it sparingly for the winter cover of precious plants. There was a small light let into the sloping roof, and where the roof met the floor there was another. There was a snugness and a secrecy about it that made Ella feel jealous of its occupier. Why had she and Rob not played here more often? There was already a bed of sorts that Sgarbh had put together for himself at the time of the storm – three or four boards were laid across bricks, the straw heaped on top and wadded into a mattress. On this Margaret laid blankets and covered all with tartan rug.

'Mr Alexander gave it with others to your grandfather – when they were both young men. Nothing wears like pure wool.' She touched the red and the blue, ran her finger on the yellow lines. 'The tartan is of the Hamiltons,' she said respectfully, as if Ella would not know. 'Mr Alexander is of the Clan Hamilton.'

'The loft makes a bonny bedroom, mother.'

'It's none so bad. If you can fancy the hard boards of the bed!' She said thoughtfully, half to herself, 'There's many a good bed up at the house could find a better use.'

Ella caught her breath. At the house! She could not believe her mother's daring – though what was different from choosing a black skirt and cutting it into a dress?

In the day's last light, chill, pale and still, Ella ran down to the shore to find Rob, who had left his work and vanished. He was idly tossing stones, skimming the surface thrice, altogether absorbed in the task. He turned only when she stood by his side.

'I know what you've been about, Ella Ross.'

'Why would you not?'

'You've been making the Sgarbh's nest.'

'I have.'

Rob tossed a last stone; the most skilful of all, four times it touched the water before it sank. Rob was pale; he spoke through his clenched back teeth.

'He'll bide on Innis Gharaidh for all time,' he said.

*

After the threat of that first storm, the winter was quiet. There were days so gentle that sounds from the mainland came clear to the island. The Macleans were building a new boathouse and the sound of their hammering came sharp across the water. Also the sound of Alister's singing. The light being unusually clear and translucent, the two children sat often on the cliff top in these days, looking towards the beach where the Macleans were building. They tried to name the people who came down to them from time to time, to bring what was needed or for sociability.

'There's Angus – he'll likely stay a while ... That's Annie Grant bringing Angus's dinner ...'

'They'll wed,' said Ella, in rather fatal tones, as if she saw in a vision all their life together and did not care for what she saw.

'What boy is that, Ella?'

'It's Hamish. He's to get a scholarship and go to college. Miss Christabel told me.'

The boy ran along the tideline with his dog, a merry mongrel. They envied him.

The shopping for supplies was now in the hands of George Erskine. He rowed twice a week to the mainland. Margaret did not go with him, though once or twice she had said she would do so, and then after all sent him with instructions. He was unexpectedly good about exchanging books between Miss Christabel and Ella. She wanted to like him for it, but trusted him too little. He was currying favour with Margaret, she thought, by being kind to her children; he had made Rob a kite. Once, three times, he ferried Miss Christabel herself on a Saturday afternoon when there was no school. It was only a brief visit, for the days were short. In the spring, Miss Christabel had said, she would come for longer, and then she and Ella could read together.

'If your mother makes no objection.'

'She would not,' Ella answered positively. But she was not entirely easy. She thought her mother did not treat Miss Christabel to quite the welcome she deserved – perhaps she feared that others might appreciate too well that hair and flawless skin. And perhaps Miss Christabel knew of this, for she added, 'In the easy tide I can row myself, Alister Maclean will lend me his boat.'

When Christmas was past there was the long slog through from the first of the year to the middle of March; but in that time the snowdrops came and went, the primroses showered over the cliffs, the daffodils promised, the camellias bloomed exotic and unreal in the shelter of the silent house. Now it was Sgarbh who helped to tend such treasures. His hand was not like John Maitland's hand. They had sharp words time and again, when he pruned the wrong joint, cut back too hard, lost precious seed or over-nourished some treasure. Sgarbh was quiet always after the first quick exchange, decent in his manner. Ella had watched in amazement sometimes, as he beat down his temper, replied with civility, even smiled at the old man, apologizing for his clumsy ways.

'I'll learn with time, maybe,' he would say.

'Maybe,' the gardener answered. 'Maybe not.'

Each spring, Mr Alexander's deserted house was cleaned from top to bottom, from attic to cellar. Though no one had lived under that roof all the year, none moved or spoke in those empty rooms, yet the furniture was shifted, the curtains taken down. Blankets hung out in sun and wind, carpets and rugs were brushed and beaten. All the paintwork was washed, the windows cleaned, the furniture polished after it had been washed first with warm water and vinegar; the silver was taken out of its baize-lined mahogany boxes, washed, polished, returned – the boxes themselves were polished, the brass key holes made to shine. And if all this might seem absurd, it was truly strange what creatures had found a way inside to make their homes in crannies and cracks – there had sometimes been mice, living on age-old crumbs that had somehow escaped Margaret's broom; and there were spiders, moths, various beetles, ants, the tiny red spider ramping through the conservatory where nothing remained to nourish them, and yet they lived. In the cellar there were strange moulds and fungi, feeding on damp; a toad lived there in apparent content – more than once, Margaret had put him out, but by some means totally undiscoverable, he had returned.

When all this work was done, that had to be done in spite of the various cleaning visits Margaret Ross made during the seasons, the house was closed to wait another year for the next complete holocaust. Yet every year, ever since the departure, had been a year of possible return. They could never know, as they closed the door on it, if the house would suddenly be flung into turmoil and excitement, if change in every aspect of the island life would then come upon them all . . .

Ella had thought of this ever since she could remember, but only as if she might have dreamt it all. This year it was different, for there was already change. There was the matter of the letters from the bank – coming regularly after that first delay, but still with no mention by name of Mr Alexander – only 'our client'.

And there was something more. Sgarbh came into the house with them and helped with the work; which was acceptable in one way but not by any means altogether. Ella hated to see him there, and so, she knew, did her grandfather. She thought there had been high words between him and her mother one night after she and Rob had been sent off to bed. Yet, now that Sgarbh was settled in with them on the island, even Ella began to wonder how they had ever managed without him, how they had managed even while her father was alive – for Sgarbh had twice his energy, double his determination. She began to mind less that a bed had indeed been found from one of the servants' rooms at the house, and had been carried out and manoeuvred up the ladder into the loft with much laughter and merriment on a sunny day.

'We'll see him in our own home any day,' said Rob. 'Shall we have a bet on it, Ella?'

'Betting's sinful,' said Ella quickly. She wanted to forget what he had said.

One spotless afternoon in mid-April, Ella had been set to the tedious task of cutting the dead blooms off the great bed of polyanthus that spread across the front of the house. She was a long time about it because she kept stopping to look at the sky, to watch the birds fly over; and to think of a story she had read in one of the books Miss Christabel had lent her. It was called *Tales from Shakespeare*, there were many coloured pictures that delighted her; but best of all she had liked reading about a magician called Prospero, who lived with his daughter and his attendant spirits on an island. Ella imagined herself the girl, who had never seen any of her own kind save her father, and then had fallen in love with a shipwrecked prince. Once or twice in the course of her work that afternoon, Ella went thoughtfully to the cliff edge and looked down upon the shore, where the tide was out and the sand just right for a stranded hero to be lying. But she saw only heaps of seaweed and a seal swimming lazily in the little bay.

The bed where Ella was working was sheltered by a low wall, no more than three feet high. Ella was all the time either crouching or kneeling at the job, and although because of the wall she could not see the house, she was aware of it quietly sleeping, gazing out of its blank windows across the matchless blue waters of the Sound, lonely and waiting. When she was a year or two younger, Ella had not liked being too near the house unless Rob were with her. There was nothing malign or threatening about it, but its patient sadness seemed over-whelming.

At the end of that afternoon, Ella heard her mother calling them all in to their tea. She collected up the last dead heads into her basket along with her knife and shears. As she straightened herself, she faced the house, standing, because of the swoop of the ground, a little elevated, so that she had an impression of seeing right into the rooms, where the late afternoon light slanted and shone richly. Alongside the front door was the dining-room, with its big bay window, the oval table that Margaret polished and polished, the great sideboard against the far wall, with above it an immense gilt-framed picture of storm at sea. Soon the shutters would be closed against the stronger sun of summertime, but in winter and spring her mother insisted that the light be let in, almost as if she feared that darkness might kill the place.

'Mr Alexander would not want it should look un-lived in,' Margaret had once said.

Who could possibly dwell there, unless it were Mrs Alexander's beautiful ghost? Sometimes Ella did gaze towards the house as if she expected to see some movement – a white hand tweaking at a curtain, or a pale face fleetingly peering from an upper window ...

And now, as she stood up and prepared to answer her mother's call, Ella knew that within the house there had been some movement. The long shaft of sunlight striking in from the western horizon, had been broken by a shadow crossing it and then re-crossing.

She froze. The breath seemed to be whisked right out of her body and for a second she hardly knew where she was. She dared not look back at the house in case she saw what had moved, but stared at her own feet in terror ... Then it was as if the blood started to flow again through her body, she took a great deep breath and then shivered.

Her grandfather, too, had heard Margaret's call, and he was passing on the far side of the lawn. He waved to Ella. At the very same instant, Ella saw Sgarbh walking round from the back of the house with a bucket in one hand and a couple of wet cloths in the other. He was level with Ella before she was able to move.

'I have been washing over the cellar steps,' he said as he passed her, not pausing in any friendly way to walk with her to the cottage. 'It is a hard task for a woman.'

Relief and confusion took their turn in Ella's mind. No ghost, then, moving in the silent house; only George Erskine about a domestic task. But if he had been cleaning the cellar steps why should she be so sure that something or someone had moved in the big dining-room? ...

She heard her grandfather speak. He had checked Sgarbh on his way to the cottage. As she went towards them, Ella saw that Granda was angry as she had never seen him, that he was shaking with rage.

'You have been in the house, George Erskine.'

'I have. And for a good purpose.'

'The house is not for you to enter alone, whatever the purpose. It is Mr Alexander's house. I am trusted to preserve it as he left it – as he would wish to see it on his return. I'll have no stranger trampling and fingering.'

'Fingering?' repeated Sgarbh.

'Aye. I said fingering. It was my meaning. Keep your hands to yourself and yourself this side the threshhold. Am I clearly understood?'

'You do make your meaning clear to me, sir.'

'Then hand me the keys.'

'It was Mistress Ross gave me the keys – will I not return them into her hand?'

'When she needs them next, she shall ask for them.'

Ella watched and listened, afraid to stay, afraid to go. Her grandfather, in his rage, looked noble enough in his face, his fine eyes flashing over his beard; but bodily he seemed to her suddenly to have become pitifully frail. She saw how Sgarbh appeared to tower above him, not because he was by any means a tall man, but because he was so immensely strong. Not for the first time, his strength seemed threatening. Yet he did take the keys of the house from his pocket, where they must have weighed very heavy, and place them deliberately in the old man's outstretched palm. In his turn, he handed them to Ella, saying as if to soften his anger, 'Well, well – it is best they hang as usual behind the kitchen door.'

Margaret called again, her voice clear in the quiet. At once, both men moved. Ella took her grandfather's hand.

'Come away in, Granda! That's twice she called!'

He responded at once, smiling quickly at her, laying his arm across her shoulders and moving off with her towards home. To her horror she felt his hand trembling as it touched her. As they went together to the open door and all things familiar that lay beyond it, Ella knew that for the first time Granda was not comforting her – she was comforting him.

5

On a calm Saturday towards the ending of the spring, if that is a time that may be named precisely, Miss Christabel rowed herself to the island. It would have been a perfect visit if only the weather had not suddenly roughened, when it was obvious the return journey would be hard going. Miss Christabel said she was strong and able, and had handled a boat since childhood in her own home.

'It was a loch you dwelt by,' someone said.

'It was – but a loch of the size that's no fish pond!'

In spite of her protests, she was rowed back to the mainland by Sgarbh, towing home Alister's boat that she had borrowed for the outward journey.

'Miss Christabel was vexed,' said Rob.

Ella did not answer. Her mother's vexation troubled her more. Margaret had greeted the visitor very kindly, as if putting aside any doubts she had had in the previous autumn, but she spoke a rather cold farewell. It would all be to do again, Ella thought. And she stood watching the departing boat with anxiety and disappointment swelling in her throat.

'It's none so terrible,' Rob said, seeing how things were with her, and aware of his mother's manner. 'Och, give over, Ella Ross. It's only the schoolmistress. She's nothing to us, since we never were let go to her school.'

'It's *not* "only the schoolmistress"!' Ella shouted, giving him a shove that threw him off his balance and sent him seat-

57

first into the nearest bush. 'She's a friend! She's a friend!'

Rob picked himself up, grumbling and offended, and Ella rushed away with her misery.

But two Saturdays later, Miss Christabel came again. Ella had watched hopefully each Saturday, and when she saw the boat at last her heart leapt up and she called to Rob to come quickly. It was the best possible day for a visit, for Sgarbh was off and away on some matters of his own.

'Who's with her?' Rob said, staring. 'That's never Alister Maclean?'

Ella shook her head. She could not yet see who was handling the oars, but whoever it was had a fine, powerful stroke.

'It's a wee boy!' cried Rob.

'It's no a wee boy at all. I see now it's Hamish Macmillan. He's twice your size and more, I wonder he'll come here at all, seeing the awful way you bloodied his nose at the funeral . . . Come on down the beach, Rob – quick!' But then she changed her mind. 'You go on. I'll run tell Mam.'

She went at a great rate to the cottage. Her mother was sitting outside on the bench in the sun, knitting furiously.

'Mother,' cried Ella, breathless, 'Miss Christabel's come again, and she has Hamish Macmillan come with her for boatman!'

'Well, now,' said Margaret. The knitting was still for a moment, then started up again, clicking in a manner that Ella was not sure promised well.

'Will there be tea enough for the two, mother?'

'I wouldn't wonder. When it comes to guests there shall always be enough. The rest must go short a little if the need be. You should know that by now, a great girl like you.'

'It is not for the tea she brought him,' Ella said. 'It is to save trouble by having someone to row her home.'

The knitting was laid aside then. Margaret reached out and took Ella's hand, saying, 'I'll be glad to see both.' She pulled Ella towards her and gave her a brief hug. 'You're a good lass,' she said; then thrust her away quickly, saying she would get indoors and see what was to be had, and if need be she'd bake a quick batch of scones, and they could open a jar of the quince jelly.

Margaret was not much given to embracing either of her children, and maybe had not done so once since the funeral all those months ago – Ella did not know whether she was more pleased or embarrassed by her mother's gesture ...

Miss Christabel was just stepping ashore by the time Ella reached the beach. Rob was making much of helping to drag the boat up the shingle strip and lodging it against the incoming tide.

'Good afternoon, Ella,' said Miss Christabel. 'You see I have a boatman of my own today. It is Hamish Macmillan, and you know him already.'

'She does,' agreed Hamish, but politely.

'And you know Ella's brother, Rob, Hamish,' cried Miss Christabel, 'for I remember well hearing how he blacked your eye.'

'It was my nose he bloodied,' said Hamish. Very courteously he added, 'I have long ago forgotten.'

It was early afternoon. It might not always be so on a Saturday, but today Ella and Rob were free of tasks about the garden island. The sun was warm, the sea sparkled, small white clouds raced with the gulls. Not only the season made it seem like a day of beginnings. From the start, from the very first moment of her arrival there with them, Miss Christabel was in a merry mood. She was so unlike the village schoolmistress of a child's imagining that Ella wondered had she fallen under some enchantment? Might she vanish when the sun set? Was she a princess just for the day? But she was better than that – a beautiful elder sister whose mood spread magic over everything.

'I need shells,' she was saying. 'Hundreds and hundreds of shells. I am showing the little girls how to make shell boxes. Will you help me, Ella, if you please? They must not be too big, they must not be too small. They must not be chipped or worn by the sea. They must be of a size – and perfect! The boys'll maybe search, too. Will you do that for me, Rob? Hamish, will you give a hand?'

How could anyone have refused her?

'Your boots'll get sopped, miss!' cried Rob.

'They will! But I shall have them off!'

With no more hesitation, Miss Christabel sat herself down on a near-by rock and pulled off her boots and stockings. Ella could hardly believe her eyes – that any grown-up person should behave so freely – and the schoolmistress, at that ... She looked round anxiously for the boys, but with perfect good manners they had moved a pace or two, and stood with their backs discreetly turned. Like them, Ella was already barefoot. She took up Miss Christabel's boots and set them, the stockings stuffed inside, on the higher rocks where no tide would touch them. Then Miss Christabel seized Ella's hand, and they ran along the sands together, the boys after them. It was like a dream, like a tale told of four people on the bright shore, four people for whom nothing unpleasant threatened, whose lives could only be packed with delights and prizes, and all of them richly deserved.

Soon they had collected scores of shells, and the scores grew into hundreds – not too big, not too small, not chipped, not worn by the sea. They piled them in the bottom of the boat for the time being.

'We'll loan you a basket, Miss Christabel,' said Ella, 'and then you must come another day to give it back!'

'I will do that!' agreed Miss Christabel.

The sun was now letting itself down a little towards the sea, and the day that was almost the last in May chilled to an evening with even a hint of frosty green along the northern horizon. Miss Christabel put on her stockings and boots and became calm and more like an ordinary mortal, more like a polite visitor, more like, in fact, the village school teacher. She went up the path with Rob, and Ella went next, then Hamish. She would have talked to him if she could have thought of anything to say. At the very last moment she managed to ask him was it true he'd be away to St Andrews one day soon?

'No, no!' he cried. 'I'm no that clever.'

'Miss Christabel says so. She says you are clever.'

'No, no!' cried Hamish again, even more firmly. 'I am not. It is not so.'

Ella was half disappointed, half pleased that if he was really clever he was too modest to admit it.

'Will it be the fishing, then?' she asked.

'Maybe. Maybe not.' He seemed to ponder what to tell her. As they talked they had fallen behind the rest, who had already reached the cottage. 'There's none else but me to earn for my mother and sisters,' he said at last, speaking low, as if he feared to be overheard. 'I am let stay one more year at the school, but I work when I may.'

He seemed to Ella as grown and purposeful as any other man on the mainland must be. He was only a few months older than she was, and that was late for the only son of a fisherman's widow to be at school. She liked to think of him diligently working for his mother, and the girls she knew only by sight and name – Bessie and Eileen.

'My cousin Dougal takes me in the boat for night fishing,' he said, more easily now. 'Then I have fish and any few pence he can spare. Also, when the supplies come in down the loch – I am there with the boat.'

'Alister's boat, is it?'

'Aye. Alister's. He has always been the one till now – there are goods to be rowed round the headland, you well know, to those that live along that shore. Alister spares me the money for that work.'

'He has a generous nature.'

'He has. And in summer, if there should be visitors, then maybe I'll have the rowing of them. He says so. Though I'll not be let as far as the lighthouse.'

'It is none so bad,' she said. 'But what if you might choose?'

Hamish did not answer at once. He looked at her with a brief, withdrawn smile and shook his head. Only as they came near enough to hear Margaret greeting Miss Christabel, and Granda joining in, did he say in a low voice, 'I'd choose to be like John Maitland.'

'How – like? Do you mean – a gardener?'

'Aye,' said Hamish, nodding now and smiling more widely. 'I'd like fine to be a gardener. Innis Gharaidh is surely the most beautiful place on earth.'

Then the picture in Ella's mind changed. She saw Hamish seated at table with them daily, she saw Granda teaching him; she saw Sgarbh no longer needed, going away – and only her mother among them all with any regrets. But Hamish would not want to be a gardener on Innis Gharaidh for ever – there must be other gardens, more to learn – there were surely gardeners required even by kings and queens ... Strange visions then chased through Ella's mind, crowded into a second as dreams are crowded before the moment of waking – how she, too, might go away, how her life need not always be an island life. She would be much older very soon, she told herself. In a few years she would be a girl waiting for some man to marry her. She would go away and live in some other place with her husband, and have children to care for ... She sent such thoughts packing, for they were at present in every way more alarming than alluring. For how could she ever leave Granda, who was first of all to her? Then she turned even from her own question, for its answer was all too plain. If she went away from the island it could only be because Granda had grown too old to stay with them any longer, and she was never able to think of him dying like all other old men.

'Here is Hamish Macmillan, Mrs Ross,' Miss Christabel was saying as he stepped inside. 'He is my prize pupil – but today he is my boatman.'

'Come away in, Hamish,' said Margaret. 'Is your mother well?'

'Thank you, she is well,' replied Hamish. 'If I should see you, I was to say she hopes I am no bother to you.'

Margaret laughed and went to make the tea. Only as her mother turned from the open door to the hearth did Ella see the laid table. While they ran along the shore a feast had been set for them. There was the best damask cloth spread, that had been given to Margaret's mother by Mrs Alexander herself and stayed mostly folded in a drawer. There were the fresh made scones, butter that Ella called real butter, that was bought on the mainland and had never seen goats' milk; there was a dish of ham finely sliced, and jars of different pickle to eat with it, and the quince jelly as promised; and last of all the one plum cake left from last Christmas, rich and dark and still moist because of the damson wine poured into it from time to time since its making.

Rob muttered, 'Losh ...' And sat down quickly lest it should all vanish before he had time to set to.

'It is my birthday,' said Miss Christabel, 'but how should Mistress Ross know of it?'

It was the final touch of magic for Ella. Miss Christabel, of her own wish, had brought her birthday to share with them ...

'Our best good wishes to you, then, Miss Christabel,' said Granda. 'If I'd a dram to hand I'd be raising my glass. Good health to you.'

'Thank you, Mr Maitland. I wish good health to you, also.'

'It is the best birthday tea ever!' cried Ella. 'It is best because it is a surprise!'

'I have a second surprise to come,' Miss Christabel said. 'A surprise even though I have been told about it! The schoolchildren are giving me a birthday party, also – a week late, but no matter. It is next Saturday afternoon and a fine tea will be laid in the schoolroom. Mrs Ross, I came most particularly to ask if Ella and Rob may be there. And you know well you would be most welcome yourself.'

'No, no!' cried Margaret. 'I was never a body for parties. As for the children ... What would you say, father?'

Ella hardly breathed. She did not know whether or not she wanted Granda to say *Yes*, for *No* might on the whole be easier. Her memories of the mainland children at Lizzie Best's on the day of the funeral clouded her mind and filled her with doubts, half spoiling the happiness of this present occasion. She seemed to see and hear and feel the shyness that must come upon her when she stood again with those mocking girls and boys.

'Why not? Why not?' said Granda. 'How does it seem to the laddie there?' he asked, nodding towards Hamish.

'I would ask Alister's boat to fetch and carry them home,' he said.

'There now, that's settled,' said Miss Christabel, smiling round the table. 'Three o'clock at the school, then, next Saturday afternoon.'

It took only a few hours from Miss Christabel's visit to remind Ella that she had no party dress.

'I've no true dress at all!' she cried. 'Only the black funeral frock! I canna wear black to a birthday party!'

Margaret frowned and quite lost her colour. 'May I be forgiven! What do you think of me, father? I clean forgot.'

'I saw you did,' he answered, with some irony in his tone.

'They've no call to be jigging off to parties at all – with their father not yet a year in his grave. Dear me, dear me – I'm a sorry sort of mourner! Now what'll I say to Miss Christabel?'

'Are we not to go?' asked Ella, crushed, even though she had not been certain of her own wishes.

'What seems best to you, father?'

'Let them go – who's to say they should not? They've little enough jaunting. Tie a black ribbon on her sleeve.'

'Aye. I'll do that.'

'What sleeve?' asked Ella.

'We'll see,' was all that Margaret said then.

The next day being Sunday there was no work, only some yawning. When the dinner was done and the dishes washed, Margaret told Ella to come with her to the house. She took the bunch of keys now back on its hook near the kitchen door and they crossed to the house over the well-mown lawn in silence. Then once again they went up the broad stair, and stood before Mrs Alexander's wardrobe; once again the key was turned in the lock and the doors opened. This time they sought among the light and billowy dresses, tucked and frilled, beautiful; long, long out of fashion.

'I can easy cut one down and make it plainer,' Margaret said.

Ella wished she need not. How fine it would be to wear the long drifting skirts, to feel them trailing behind her. She would pick up the folds in front, knowing certainly that she looked like the princesses with golden braided hair in the pictures that adorned the borrowed books of fairy tales. Everyone would turn to look after her. 'It is the Princess Ella. She dwells on an enchanted island and all the princes in the land seek her in marriage ...'

'This, now,' said Margaret. She held out two dresses, one a deep rose colour with ribbon-work at the neck, the other a near-lavender.

'Which?' Ella asked, her heart beating for the rose.

'The mauve silk, Ella. There's none to look scorn, then – it is half mourning, and well enough for one of your age after the months gone.'

'Will I wear the black ribbon?'

'Maybe. Maybe not.'

'Not,' prayed Ella silently, watching the beautiful rosy gown being put back in its place and the doors closed, locked ...

They were leaving the house when Margaret paused.

'I'll take some of the table silver home to polish ...'

Somehow Ella knew that her mother intended in this way to compensate by extra care for what she had taken from Mrs Alexander's clothes closet. She waited in the hall while Margaret turned back into the dining-room. In the hall were many pictures, of stags and hares and duck, and other sad animals dead at the hunter's feet or laid on the kitchen table waiting for the cook's knife. The fur of the hare was so real that Ella would have liked to stroke it, and just as real was the red of its oozing life blood. Ella was used enough to animals dead or dying, taken for the pot or injured and needing dispatch. But the picture made her turn away. She looked around for something gentler, but there was so much death – even the glass case of bright stuffed birds that had delighted her as a small child now showed itself to her as a case of birds that had once flown, and then been halted in their flight.

Ella heard her mother fumbling with the keys and the sound

of the drawer pulled open. She sat down on the big settle and amused herself by sliding its polished length two or three times. The drawer closed with a thud and her mother came out of the dining-room.

'I'll carry it,' Ella said.

But Margaret's hands were empty. She said she would do the polishing another day after all; it was not so long since it had been done. They left the house and locked the door behind them. They carried the dress back to the cottage. Ella skipped now and then and asked questions about the dress – how would it be cut, should they not leave the wide lace collar that was so pretty? Her mother answered absently and at last cried out that she should not pester. Surprised, Ella saw that Margaret was pale. Her eyes looked anxious, her mouth was very firm-set.

It was then that Ella remembered.

'He was there that day,' Ella said to Rob. 'He was in the house, and Granda saw him and was angry. He took the keys away from him.'

'It's the first you ever said of it.'

'I wished not to think of it, Rob. But I am thinking now.'

'Aye,' said Rob, 'and I am thinking, too.'

There had been some soft drizzle, on and off, during that Sunday, but now the sky had cleared to a fierce sharp blue, with below it the sea mirroring the brightness. The sun was hot as the brother and sister sat together in their secret place on the cliff shelf.

'Tell me what you are thinking.'

'I am thinking the drawer was empty and the silver gone, gone with Sgarbh.'

'I am thinking the same, Rob.'

There was a pause. Then Rob said on a long exploding breath, 'If it's so, Ella, he'll no come back to Innis Gharaidh.'

'Poor Mr Alexander's silver forks and spoons!'

'We'll see them no more,' said Rob, cheerfully.

All the same, at noon the next day, Sgarbh returned without

any signs of guilt to the island that seemed to have become accepted as his home.

The lavender silk was a dress that Ella could enjoy. Its soft folds hung gently, and even without a fine long looking-glass, like those up at the house, she could see she was a girl – in the jerseys that she wore mostly she had no shape at all. If only her hair had more gold in it, like Miss Christabel's, like the princesses', she would not have minded her appearance. Though it was altered a great deal, and skilfully, the dress still had its wide lace collar.

'Wear this,' said her mother, as Ella swished the folds this way and that. Margaret had a long black sash in her hand.

'Oh *no!*' cried Ella. 'It's fine as it is!'

'You'll do as I bid, for decency's sake. It will be expected.'

There was more in her mother's voice than the stark firmness Ella was well accustomed to. Margaret sounded harsh, almost distracted. And so maybe she was, knowing what no other knew save one. Would she speak of it? Ella knew she would not.

The black sash cut the dress in two. From seeing herself clad in floating flowing beauty, Ella found she was made into a bag of flour tied round the middle. Rebellion stirred. She had not thought, till now, that she might not always do what her mother wished her to do. It surprised and slightly shocked her to know that she would have the sash off before ever she set foot in the schoolroom. It was because of some change that Ella could not have put a name to – perhaps, suddenly knowing her mother to be less than perfect, she saw no reason why she must strive to be perfect herself.

Things were much worse for Rob. It was now altogether impossible for him to wear the knickerbocker suit he had worn with so much loathing and discomfort to the funeral.

'It must be the jacket with your kilt, there's no other way,' said Margaret. 'Will you look at the size of him, father?' She gave him a displeased shove away from her in her worry. 'You've been eating too well, Robert. I'll see there's less oats to your porridge from now on!'

67

'I'll stay behind,' said Rob. 'I canna be seen. They'll all laugh.'

'You will go as invited. Into your jacket, now, and let me see how it looks.'

It would not do up. When Saturday came Rob could only go in his best jersey and the kilt that had belonged to that other boy who had once lived on this island. They were clothes too hot for the day. His face began to shine no more than a few yards from home.

Hamish came as he had promised. Ella and Rob met him on the shore. They each carried a posy for Miss Christabel that Granda had picked and tied. Hamish had his jacket rolled carefully in the bottom of the boat. It was his cousin Graham's, he said, who had grown out of it. Meanwhile his cousin Graham's waistcoat, three sizes too big, flapped around him as he rowed. Ella wanted to laugh, but remembered Rob's fear of being laughed at for a jacket not too big but too small. And who was she, who had had no dress of her own, to laugh at a boy for borrowing from his cousin? The neatness of his shirt beneath the great waistcoat, that showed careful darns and patches as he rowed, moved her to a warm sympathy. She smiled at him and he smiled back. If only he had been some nice familiar collie dog, she would have stroked him very kindly and with great pleasure to herself...

The schoolroom when they reached it was unlike any schoolroom that Ella could ever have imagined. It was decked out with coloured paper chains and toy balloons, and on every high window-sill there were jam jars full of flowers – pinks and daisies and buttercups, with here and there a few roses – all set among branches of broom picked off the headland. There was music – Lizzie Best at the harmonium in the corner. She stopped playing when she saw Ella and Rob, and held out her hands to them.

'How's your mother? Tell her it's time she came visiting. Is your grandfather well? That's a pretty dress you're wearing, Ella. Quite the young lady!'

Did she recognize it, Ella wondered, since she had looked after the beautiful Mrs Alexander all those years ago? Perhaps she would speak of it when she met Ella's mother. 'What a pity, Margaret,' she might say, 'that Ella's lovely lavender silk dress – so like a dress of Mrs Alexander's that I remember well – had no decent black sash worn for her father's sake ...' For by now the sash was rolled up tightly and Hamish had taken it for safety into his jacket pocket.

'Ella!' cried Miss Christabel, coming in her turn to greet them. 'How grown up you look!'

'It is my favourite dress,' said Ella, as if she had a great closet crammed full of such things, 'but I have not worn it till this day.' She held out her posy. 'From Granda. And Rob has one for you.'

Miss Christabel took a posy in each hand and showed them round the room to the other children. They all stared at Ella and there seemed not a face in sight that she had ever seen before. She could not even be certain of Hamish's two sisters. And now Hamish himself had joined the other boys and Rob had gone with him, only girls were left at Ella's end of the room. Then the dress was no longer enough. She wished the party could be over. She did not know where to look or what to do or where to put her hands. She wished they might all go home.

At tea, when they went scuttling for places, the boys all sat together and left the girls to cluster about Miss Christabel's end of the table. Ella was seated next to Miss Christabel, but she no longer found anything to say. On Ella's other side sat a big girl called Alison; maybe she was Alison Grant and maybe Alison Murdoch – Ella could not know. Like most of the girls, Alison wore a white frilled pinafore stiff with starch. Ella's dress was the finest there, but all she longed for now was a pinafore.

'I'd not care to be living on Mr Alexander's island,' said Alison in a low voice, in Ella's right ear.

'Would you not?' said Ella, staring in her turn. 'Why would that be?'

'I have heard of him.'

'How would you not – if you know it is his island?'

'He is dead now,' said Alison.

Ella went red. 'No. He is not.'

'Aye – he's dead. I heard my Mam say so. Good riddance, then, she said. We'll no see him again, she said. And Maggie Ogilvie was there and said, No, we'll no see him again, she said. She was very glad.'

This was so extraordinary to Ella that she wondered if Alison was perhaps a mad girl and did not know what she was saying. But she looked altogether too bright, her rather small eyes very sharp and her mouth pursed in disapproval.

'I cannot tell what it is you are talking about,' said Ella. She turned away from Alison, hoping Miss Christabel might rescue her. But Miss Christabel was busy with a child on her other side who had spread jam all about her face and fingers.

Alison leant close and cupped her hands round her mouth making them into a trumpet through which what she whispered would be sure to fall into Ella's cringing ear.

'He killed his only son,' she said.

Afterwards, Ella could not recall if she answered Alison. She thought not. But even if she spoke one word, there was no more to it. She turned her shoulder to Alison and began gabbling so hard and loud that Miss Christabel was bound to turn from her other neighbour. At the sound of Ella's strange voice and unexpected chatter sweeping away her tongue-tied silence, Miss Christabel looked at first surprised, then faintly uneasy, then at last quite anxious. She thought maybe Ella wished to leave the table and could not quite bring herself to ask. But it was not that at all. It was simply that Ella, reeling from Alison's outrageous remarks, dared not allow a silence in which she would have to think of them. All through the rest of the afternoon she behaved so wildly and so unlike herself that not only Miss Christabel but also Lizzie Best asked her was she quite well.

At last it was time to say good-bye and thank you and go home. Hamish and Ella and Rob left together and walked down to the shore where Alister's boat would be waiting.

'I have forgot the basket!' he cried, when they were almost there. 'That you loaned Miss Christabel for the shells. I'll not be a minute fetching it.'

He turned at once and ran back, and they went on ahead. As if everything had changed and settled to a bad pattern, they found Sgarbh there, waiting with the island boat, *Roin*.

'Jump in,' he said. 'I came for the groceries and stayed for you.' He was smiling and friendly, but they held back in distaste and disappointment. So then he said, unsmiling, 'I am waiting.'

'Hamish is coming,' said Rob, desperate.

'There's no need of Hamish since I'm here myself. Waste no more of my time.'

There was nothing for it but to do as he bid them. The boat pulled away, and then they saw Hamish running with the basket in his hand. Worse, Ella realized that the black sash was still in his pocket. The whole day had become terrible. Now she had to think about what Alison had said, and as soon as possible she was telling Rob.

'The girl's a great liar,' said Rob.

'What shall we do? Must we tell Granda?'

'Aye, we should do that. We should tell Granda,' he answered positively.

For two or three days they did attempt to draw their grandfather aside and tell him what Alison had said. But it never seemed the right moment. They could not get him alone, or if they did there was not enough time to speak of a thing so terrible, and anyway it was hard to find the words. Between themselves they spoke of it all the time, in every minute that they were together, wondering, inventing, puzzled and anxious. For if Alison had indeed heard such things, then on the mainland they must surely know another Mr Alexander. Maybe Alison was after all a shade simple – or merely malicious. Would Miss Christabel be able to help them? Should they speak of it first to her? Ella would have liked this but Rob was all against it.

'If she came next Saturday – should we not speak to her?'

'She will not come this week,' Rob answered. 'It will be the next one after.'

Their time ran increasingly from Saturday to Saturday, because of Miss Christabel, because of Hamish; because, too, their grandfather had lately seemed willing to let them free of work on that afternoon of the week.

'We must not tell Granda save in the right words, Rob. He might drop to the ground from the shock of it.'

All this greatly upset them, and also the fact that they had had no chance to explain to Hamish before Sgarbh whipped them into the boat and carried them away. Rob was sure Hamish must understand, but Ella all but wept from fear of losing him for a friend. She was forever looking out over the water, hoping that she might see him rowing towards the island – for there was still the basket, and the sash. The loss of the sash had greatly angered her mother.

In spite of Rob's certainty, Ella was looking for Miss Christabel and Hamish when next Saturday came. She had been sent to pick flowers for the cottage. She was stooping to pick a good bunch of violas from the bed near the house, and when she stood up and looked out she saw Hamish at last. But he was rowing away from the island. He must have dumped the basket and, it was to be hoped, the sash also, and rowed away fast, because he no longer wished to speak with them.

In black sorrow and disappointment, Ella rushed to find Rob.

'It was Hamish! He has come and he has gone! Come quick to the beach and see has he left any message!'

There was nothing but the basket, the sash laid in it, and a pattern of footsteps across the sand, over which the returning tide was already washing, carrying away all such blemishes.

There was one thing strange about this. Not that Hamish had come and gone, not that he had left them what was theirs. The strange thing was that there were two sets of footprints – but there had been only Hamish in the boat rowing steadily back to the mainland.

6

Ella stood very still, gazing down at the footprints. She thought of mermen and sea serpents, of monsters that rise from the deep, of pirates and wreckers and sea robbers of every sort. A cold, unseen hand brushed her cheek and she shivered.

Rob said, 'Hamish put on his boots.'

At once the magic creatures and the marauders were diminished. Truly the prints were of a boy's foot – but one string barefoot with toes curling and sinking in the sand, the other with a leather sole and heel.

'He would not,' said Ella. 'You know well he would not come rowing in his boots.'

'He put them on when he stepped out.'

'But those are Hamish's feet – the bare ones. Have you never thought he has a very big big toe?'

Rob had not, but he frowned. He looked quickly at Ella and she knew that he, too, had felt that chilly twinge which had now returned to trouble her.

'Then it was another laddie came with Hamish, Ella.'

'There was none but Hamish in the boat, I tell you.'

'You would not see him if he should be lying down ...'

'What if there should be someone left behind, Rob ... ?'

'There would be footprints leading away.'

She looked hastily around, but the sea had already scooped and scalloped along the edge of the little bay. If there had indeed been more prints leading inland they were well and truly washed out, for the tide, though it had left Rob and Ella standing on a dry scoop, had already reached the shingle behind them. Someone might have walked from the boat to the rocks and vanished that way, but there was no sign left. Even as they spoke of it, the sea washed forward and covered their own feet, taking with it the last of the prints, Hamish's and that other's. Ella and Rob were obliged to step back and make their way towards the cliff path.

Above them the garden island swept its gentle curve from the small bay, mounting gracefully to that high part, rock guarded, that seemed to match the pattern of the mainland cliffs. There shepherds had once kept snug in small huts, and then had built a more proper house – the house that Mr Alexander had turned to size and splendour. The time of year had filled the garden with colour, had swept in its own tide over the island which suddenly seemed to Ella strange and almost unreal. For the first time she saw it as a different world from the mainland, where ordinary people lived, people like Hamish Macmillan, like Miss Christabel, who knew nothing of the curious imprisonment of being circled by the sea's uneasy and mysterious waters. Dwellers in such places were indeed captive, bound by a rhythm which, if one beat were missed, must play right round the clock before regaining its true tempo. Miss a tide and it was possible to lose a whole day's living.

As Ella turned for home, carrying almost reluctantly the basket that Hamish had silently left for her, she felt lost and puzzled, but could not understand what she was feeling. It was as if she wondered where her feet were carrying her, as if she expected their prints to be washed away, as those on the shore had been washed, so that none could know who was Ella Ross, or what her heart had held . . .

She went back to the flowers she had left tossed down on the grass when she ran off to find Rob. Some had already wilted in the sun and she looked for others. On the far side of the house she could see her grandfather gingerly hoeing among seedlings only a week or so planted out. There was no sign of Sgarbh; maybe he was in the walled garden, or maybe he was with her mother, somewhere out of sight. With bewilderment and fright touching her so strangely, Ella longed for help and knew no way of seeking it. Miss Christabel's books had freed and stimulated her imagination, then set it in a turmoil. Her life seemed filled with sudden puzzles – they had come upon her like arrows shot from behind a hedge. First there had been the arrival of Sgarbh, then the unwelcome certainty that her mother leant towards him more, even, than Ella cared to admit, that she had known him before he began to work on the island. Then the knowledge that her grandfather was growing old and not quite well and with doubts of his own; the extraordinary words that fat Alison had dropped breathily into her flinching ear – and now the footprints, which seemed to her almost like a chain linking all the rest.

If only it could have been a day for Miss Christabel to come calling! But she had much to do just then, the school term ending, with little notes to parents, the school tea, the giving of prizes. In fact at this time everyone was busy – there was hay to be got in before the weather thought of breaking; their own fields must be cut, too, here on the island. They had not so much as all that, but it was always a long business, turning green grass into dry hay ...

Her grandfather must have seen her sitting back on her heels, the flowers she had picked lying untidily in her lap. He came towards her, carrying his hoe over his shoulder and asked her, smiling into his beard, had the fine day tired her.

'Granda,' said Ella, her voice shaking, 'a girl called Alison says Mr Alexander is dead.'

He paused no more than a second before asking, 'What girl would that be?'

'A fat girl, Granda. At Miss Christabel's birthday party.'

He swung his hoe from his shoulder and stood leaning upon it, looking down at her. Now she had spoken she was frightened, for she knew there was no going back – she must tell all and hear all, and she and Rob had agreed it was enough to make the old man's heart stop its beat.

'We must have heard of it,' he said, not casting the idea away as he had done in the past. 'How should we not? We have the

75

money coming as ever. Except ...' He was considering that slight change in the words of the letter that came with the money; she could see him puzzling over it. 'I have thought and troubled myself over this, Ella,' he said, as if he were speaking to someone much older. 'But your mother was right. If it should be that Mr Alexander had died, but had maybe left in his will that the money should still be sent – then there would be some lawyer writing to tell us of the matter. It could only be so.'

'It could,' agreed Ella, knowing nothing of such things but wanting to please him.

'Come away in,' he said. 'Pick up your flowers. I am tired, too.' As they walked away together he said, 'Those on the mainland have ever laid their tongues maliciously about the name of Mr Alexander.'

'Why would they?'

'The island was long let lie idle. None cared to work it till he came to the place to live. But then it was said he had taken it from the sheep.'

'He had not!'

'He had not – but that is the way the world goes, my lassie. You are too young to know of it.' He paused a moment, standing there looking at her closely, frowning slighly. 'Did she say more—yon Alison?'

'Aye, she did.'

'What more?'

Ella hesitated. She would never find the word.

'Granda, it is too bad to tell.'

He sighed, saying again, 'Come away indoors. We'll sit quiet and you must tell me.'

Ella longed for her words back, but it was too late. She went with her grandfather, and her mother was in the house alone after all, with a basket of mending beside her. She looked up as they came in, and laid her work by at once, saying, 'Sit in your chair, father. You are tired.'

He sank down, letting out a great sigh. 'I am not tired by work but by what Ella has told me – that a fat lass at the tea-party said that the Laird has died.'

76

Margaret looked sharply from one to the other, then seemed to decide what she must say.

'I know they are talking in this manner. Lizzie Best spoke of it to me. It is because last winter the letter was so long in coming. They know fine about quarter days and the envelope with its postmark from Edinburgh. What else are they to talk about unless it is such small matters?'

'Small...?'

'They are bound to gossip, father – that is small ... What did the lass tell you, Ella?'

'That he was dead.'

'How did she know it, then?'

'She heard her mother tell it. And say – and say *Good riddance*!'

'Ah,' said John Maitland; it was a long-drawn, wounded sound. 'What more?'

'Mother, must I say?'

'Yes. You must.'

'That he – that he had killed his only son!'

It sounded at once worse, gabbled as she had gabbled it, and most ridiculous. Ella bit her lip and nervously half smiled at the words. But the protests, scornful or angry, which she had expected to hear did not in fact come.

'I told you,' Margaret said in a low voice, 'that Mr Alexander's son was dead.'

'You said – an accident ...'

'So it was – so it was. An accident! A terrible accident! But there was ever a feeling against Mr Alexander in the village – because of the island, because it was made a garden. What was a man doing growing flowers that could have grazed twenty sheep on the land? It was ten years – ten years at the least, since sheep had grazed on the island. That's the truth as I know it from your grandfather.'

'It is the certain truth,' he agreed. 'Your grandmother that was born in the village, and her father before her, knew this.' He sat back in his chair, laying his head against it so that his beard jutted. He had closed his eyes and he spoke in a sad, a weary voice. 'This is why we cannot count friends among the mainland people, Ella – save the Macleans and one or two more. We keep ourselves to ourselves to show our scorn . . . But after so long – that such things should still be said . . . I mind well the first time I heard such talk – and it hurts me no less now that I am old.'

They were no nearer to the matter of Mr Alexander's son, no nearer to the 'accident', and Ella did not know how to speak of it again. She saw the truth being drawn away from her into hiding once more, lost in a tangle of sighs and distaste for what had been said.

'You now see,' her mother said, 'why you and Rob get kept from the village. It is for us to guard Mr Alexander's good name. Look what happens the very first time you are let visit there alone!'

'I did not answer her,' said Ella quickly; for now she felt she was in some way to blame, and must excuse herself for what she had been told. The confusion of this strange day continued, pressing upon her, and she could not tell the meaning of it any more than she could tell why there should have been two sets of footprints in the sand. She repeated her words, since neither had responded to her, 'I did not answer!'

'Best so, indeed.'

'How should I answer?' Ella cried. 'How should I know what to say?'

'There was no need to reply. You knew she was speaking dreadful lies.'

'How?' Ella insisted, her voice mounting, almost shrill. 'How would I know that?'

She saw her mother's face close on itself like a box with the lid snapped down, the key turned. Margaret was very pale. She looked at her father, and although he had not opened his eyes, he seemed to receive the look.

'Tell her, Margaret.'

'How will a child understand?'

'She's near a woman. Tell her.'

Ella saw how bitterly upset her mother was, how little she

wanted to tell this tale, whatever it might be; for with an elbow on the table edge and her hand shielding her eyes she spoke so low that at first Ella thought she might not be able to hear what was being said.

'It is a sad and bitter story, Ella. You do not need to hear it told.'

'I am fourteen years old, mother. Granda says I'm near grown up. I am!'

'Well, then ... Well, then ... Mr Alexander had just the one son, as well you know, and called after him. William. William Hamilton Alexander. His mother having died – as I have told you – he was cared for by Lizzie Best. Then Lizzie got wed to Rory Maclean. So Mr Alexander's son lived mostly here with us. He was much of an age with me. We were island children – like you and Rob. We played on the shore ...'

Such times were bound to end, she said, he being a gentleman's son with a place in the world. After he went away to school in England, some great famous school, he was on the island with his father only for holidays.

'He was always handsome. From a wee lad he had a flash in his eye. It was – it was a princely thing,' Margaret said; then looked quickly from under her hand at Ella, and half smiled at the word.

After the distant schooling he had gone to the university and then abroad. It was several years before he came to the island one day in winter, unexpectedly. It was rough weather and he had a fair tossing from the mainland.

'But he was a strong man, for all his education,' Margaret said, with some strange pride in her voice. 'Was he not very strong, father?'

'He was a very fine and upstanding man. I mind him striding up through the windy day towards his father's house, and the lass not even trying to keep up with him.'

'The lass ...?' said Ella.

Margaret did not take up the tale here but left it to her father.

'He had wed an Englishwoman, Ella,' Granda said. 'He had not told Mr Alexander his intention. Indeed in the years he was abroad he had barely written a word home, and this had angered his father without what more was to come. He brought his wife with him to tell the news for the first time – and they already a whole year wed!' He took a deep breath at the recollection of it. 'The house was like to burst with Mr Alexander's great rage and the hurt he had received from his son's neglect of him. He had had long to brood over that neglect and it came from him like lightning. Outside was the wild storm beating up the Sound – but inside, too, the tempest raged. It raged many hours. Father and son were well matched in power and fury.'

Now there was a silence. Each teller of the tale seemed to wait uncertainly for what the other might say next. Margaret rose suddenly and went to the window. She stood with her back turned and Ella knew that her hands were twisted tightly into one another.

'Young William Alexander flung from the house at last,' she said, her voice heavy with recollection. 'He would have left then and taken his wife with him – but it was a most mighty storm, a storm still remembered. He went instead to pace with his anger, no doubt, for we saw him stride by this very window.' Again she paused, and now she put her face in her hands and rocked herself as if that old grief were still upon her. 'The storm took him. The seas took him. In the dark and the wet and the great gale he slipped and fell. There were the marks of his boots, slithering ... It was long, very long before they found his poor body washed up far along the Sound.'

It was a terrible tale. Worse than any Ella could have imagined. Worse than battle, shipwreck, earthquake ...

'None ashore ever forgave Mr Alexander,' John Maitland said. 'As they had always resented him, so they were glad to accuse him. He had killed his only son, they said – aye, and I see the meaning in it well enough.'

Mr Alexander, after this tragedy, had been a man broken and demented, his whole generous nature changed by disaster; he seemed at times to have lost his reason – they had feared, even, that he might take his own life.

Ella wondered what had become of the unhappy wife who had been the innocent cause of such uproar.

'She fled as soon as the seas went down,' her grandfather said. 'I took her to Lizzie Best, and she stayed a little, then they drove her the many miles to get on a train and ride away. She was ever on Mr Alexander's conscience – and that was why he left the island at last though years had passed – for his conscience' sake he had to find her. "Keep Innis Gharaidh as I would wish it," he said. And: "Take what you need from the house ..." And every quarter day the money came but never any written word from himself. And that showed the sad change in him by reason of what had occurred – for when we were both young men he had a warm heart, greatly troubled for the injustice there is in the world.' The old man was silent, but then he said, 'But he told me also that I would hear when he found what he was seeking. The world is as big as eternity. Who knows but he is still seeking – so why do I expect any word?'

He straightened himself in his chair and looked at Ella. It was a long sad look.

'Sorrow is a great burden, lass. It makes the shoulders bent. Another man's sorrow must be shared by his friends, else he may fall under the burden.'

She nodded, not knowing what to say. A silence settled over them, broken only by outside sounds – the gulls, the sea running at a full tide, the geese conversing one to the other as they rested together like white boats at anchor on the cropped grass below the cottage door. It was a fine and pleasant evening, but the past had darkened it and torn it into tatters.

Now it was as if a book had been closed. Ella watched Granda rise and walk slowly out of the open door to sit alone on the bench against the wall. He went rather fumblingly and not quite upright, and she saw what he meant about the weight that sorrow lays upon those who must accept it.

Her mother turned from the window, filled the kettle, stirred the fire for the kettle's sake, and a peaty, consoling smell stole about the kitchen.

'After Mr Alexander left us,' Margaret said, her back still to Ella, 'all those many years gone, Wallace Ross came to help with the work. When he had been a year or so on the island, I married him.'

Then for the first time she faced her daughter, saying very clearly, 'He was different enough. He was different in every way ... Do you understand?'

'Yes, mother,' Ella said, her voice so taken from her that she nodded to make her answer plain. She did understand. The truth and the certainty of it was a flood of light in her mind. 'I do! I do!' she cried, this time loud and positive.

She wished she might hold and comfort her mother. *Mother! Mother!* she was calling inside herself. But it was too difficult to get out. She had to look away, for however awful the tale had been, it was the sadness of it that lingered for Margaret. She had lost what could only have been beyond her – the young rich man with his princely air ...

'There,' said Margaret, in her day-to-day voice. 'That story's told. Best you find the others now and say it's time to come indoors.'

Ella had thought she must tell all this to Rob at once, she could not keep it inside herself, it was surely too great and too heavy. But it was difficult to know where to begin, and so she put off the telling that evening after she had heard the tale, and then all next day. It was dry fine weather and as another week began there was plenty of work to be done. Ella's fingers resisted her and fumbled over the simplest tasks. Set to tidy the long bed running along the outside of the walled garden, she sighed and paused and yawned and stretched herself. Once she thought she saw Sgarbh watching her from the big greenhouse; he was setting in a new pane of glass where one had been cracked. It gave him excuse to peer, no doubt, and she moved away gradually out of his sight. She remembered how Hamish Macmillan would be happy to become a gardener and wished he could be there then to help her. Did he, too, believe that Mr Alexander had killed his only son? She thought he might not, since he was ready to work at the garden that had first made bad blood between the village and the island. If he ever spoke of it, might she tell him the truth? She would have to ask her mother what she should say, but she did not wish to speak to her again of the matter because of the pain it gave her. A year ago, perhaps even yesterday, Ella would not have sought to spare her mother's feelings for she would not have understood them. As she had listened to the terrible story a change had come to her – a knowledge that she would sooner have foregone. Of all the stories she had read there had been no more than two or three that ended unhappily. As her mother's had ended all those years ago. Only it had not altogether ended, since there was no book to close. It was a true life story, so it must continue until the end of life was reached.

Even working fitfully, Ella finally had a basket of rubbish, weeds and dead heads and snippings, that must be carried to the heap halfway down the path on the far shore of the island. There the rocks fell away and it was easy to scramble on the shallow slopes. The heap was carefully out of sight and every so often it was turned, and gradually the rubbish rotted down. Ella had seen Rob's head bobbing in the direction of the heap and she was glad of an excuse to go after him, for her loneliness today was hardly to be endured.

She hauled up her heavy basket and picked her way at last down to the heap. Rob had vanished now, just when she needed him. She was tipping the last bits out of the basket when she saw some movement closer to the shore, and knew that he must have played truant in this last quarter of the day. Sgarbh set lobster pots among the rocky pools, and Rob liked to go down to see what they held, and to watch with mixed feelings the sad fierce creatures imprisoned and doomed.

She was going to call out – was he coming up, or should she go down – when she saw him again.

Only it was not Rob down there on the rocks. It was another boy. A stranger.

7

Ella was unaccustomed to strangers in her life. Sgarbh had been a stranger once, and in a way remained one. And they were strangers on the mainland, for all she knew at least their family names and could mostly match name to face. But to see a stranger here on the shore, walking about below her unknowing, was like seeing a picture animated. She dropped down and crouched out of sight.

The boy, she saw now, was a good deal bigger than Rob and bigger than she was – partly by virtue of being a lad, though she thought he might not be all that much older. He had discarded his boots and stockings and his feet and legs looked strange in consequence, for he was wearing a good tweed knickerbocker suit. It was like the suit Rob had had, that had belonged first to Lizzie Best's London nephew. But such a suit, in spite of the bare legs, sat well on this boy, for he was a different sort of boy. Ella saw at once that he would not expect to find himself scrambling about in tattered grubby trousers. He had the air of some other place.

Now the footprints in Saturday's sand were explained away – the last part of his journey, however long or strange it may have been, had been with Hamish, no doubt in Alister Maclean's boat. Hamish would have left him on the shore as men have been left on distant shores by mutinous crews and pirates. Perhaps he thought this was a desert island where he could live alone – only Hamish for certain had told him differently, and he had his own two eyes to prove it. Where had he been hiding? What had he lived on? It was a poor time of year, more flower than fruit, though there were wild strawberries just beginning if he could find them. He did not look the sort to know about mussels and crabs and prawns and he would have sense enough not to raid the vegetable patch. He must have brought food with him – and that meant he had made a plan for coming here.

There was a slight movement behind her, and Ella looked round sharply, knowing it must be Rob coming and intent on silencing him. He was quick to understand her frown and her waving, dictatorial hand. He slipped down beside her, stealthy and obedient. He whispered,

'Is it the old seal?'

She shook her head and pointed. She heard his breath suck in. They squatted there together, gazing down at the stranger, who seemed content to sit on the rocks, or else to let himself down to the shore and walk there, picking up shells and holding them intently on the palm of his hand. He had rather thick straight fair hair, worn perhaps a fraction longer than Rob or Hamish and their ilk would have thought fit. The wind lifted and turned the lock that fell over his eyes.

They must have watched him half an hour before, never once glancing above where the watchers crouched, the boy moved away along the shore and vanished.

'It was Hamish brought him,' Rob said. He sounded rather relieved, as though he had feared a haunting. 'I never saw him till this.'

'He has been hiding these two days! Where would he hide, Rob?'

'In the dry cave?'

'I think so.'

'He's maybe some criminal escaped from prison,' Rob suggested.

'Whisht!' said Ella.

'Aye, he could be – and a price on his head. It would make us rich.'

'*Rob!*'

'Who, then?'

She thought of the girl in the story, the girl who had lived on an island with her magician father, of the king's son flung upon the shore ...

'How should I tell who?'

'A spy!'

'What would he be spying? He's not by any means very busy. Maybe,' she said, 'a messenger ...'

The moment she had said it she knew that she was right. He was a messenger.

'From a long way, Rob. Come about Mr Alexander ...'

'Didn't I say that? I said he was a spy!'

'It's two different things, Rob Ross.'

'A messenger come to spy, then – to see what has come to the island all these years – to know if anything has been taken from the house.'

She thought of Sgarbh, of the silver spoons and forks, and she was alarmed.

'Why would he? Why would a messenger be a spy?'

'Why would any but a spy stay hiding? It is not what messengers do in the stories you read me.'

No, indeed; in such tales they came urgently, with news of the gods, of battles; to rouse armies, to send men in armour to Troy, or to bring word of the death of some king.

'Where are you going?'

He had moved suddenly and she grabbed at him and held him.

'Granda. I'm telling Granda he's here.'

'No! Let him bide in the dry cave if he will. He cannot live there for ever. He must go round the bay for fresh water – maybe he's not found it yet. He must come out soon enough.'

'What if he should escape?'

'He has no boat.'

'We have a boat. He'll maybe steal *Roìn*.'

'I say he will not.'

'Or *Caillich*.'

'No! Come away now.'

He grumbled, but he would do as she said. Soon he might

86

know better, she knew it and even waited for it. But he was still a little boy, his habit was to obey her and he would do so now.

Ella was tingling with excitement at the thought of the stranger sharing the island, and none knowing but just the two of them. It gave her a feeling of importance and wisdom and all that evening she barely found time to speak, she was so taken up with her own thoughts. For what was to happen next? What amazing thing was about to burst upon them? Ella could not have said in the least what she expected of her skulking messenger, only that because of his mysteriously secret presence nothing could ever be the same again. She dreaded lest Sgarbh should have cause to go to the mainland and be asked who was the lad Hamish had rowed to the island – for someone must have seen him. Yet again, there had already been a few summer visitors about, and Alister's boat was always at their disposal. No doubt the stranger had sworn Hamish to secrecy – no, he would have scorned to swear, just given his word. Money would have changed hands, too, so important to Hamish with his responsibilities ... But someone was sure to inquire, not openly, since straight questions were a shade discourteous, but in some roundabout manner that was bound to set Sgarbh nosing about for the truth.

Two things struck Ella as hopeful – the general business of the season, and the fact that Lizzie Best would have her sister from England staying as was usual each summer – and when she was there they talked so much it was well known that Lizzie had words and thoughts for no one else.

The weather stayed fine and the stranger lurked still. Away over behind the house, where the island flattened out, the grass had been cut for haying, and they worked at it solidly; even Margaret joined in. So there was no one with time to wander about and discover the cave dweller. And because of this urgent work, no one left the island. This often happened in summer time when there were vegetables and eggs and plenty of goat's milk for cheese, and so much to be done that there was little energy for such matters as going to church or visiting Lizzie Best.

In the middle of the week, looking at Ella and Rob burnt by the sun, John Maitland said they should not work that afternoon. They went to hide among the rocks above what they called the dry cave, and waited hopefully for the stranger to appear. There were now a few signs of him for any with eyes sharp enough. An apple core had bobbed on a turning tide and now rested among dry seaweed high up the sandy strip. It was clear that there had been coming and going, for grass and heather had a trampled look here and there. Besides, birds in that part were restless, a jay had chattered incessantly and seagulls on the higher cliffs to westward, still with some young, had swooped and screamed so urgently that it was a miracle none had remarked it save Ella and her brother.

'He must be hungry soon,' said Ella, puzzled by the time he had managed to sustain himself.

'What if he brought food for a month – a great trunkful of it,' said Rob. 'Shall we never go seek him in the cave?' He began grumbling about 'having no right on the shore'.

'Not yet,' said Ella. 'We'll leave him bide till Sunday.'

By now she was wondering a little, trying to still a niggling fear that imagination had got the better of her – that, hot from the tragic romantic tale of Mr Alexander's son, she had made a romance of her own. Maybe there was none better in the cave below but some boy intent to camp there, or one who had run away from school.

To keep Rob quiet and to maintain her own feeling of poetry and fantasy, Ella at last told Rob the story of young William Alexander, of his awful death after the quarrel, of the flight of his poor widow and Mr Alexander's bitter remorse that had led him to leave everything and go to search for her.

'He cannot ever have found her, Ella.'

'Why do you say so?'

'When he found her – he would come home.'

She was unwilling to agree. She wanted it all to be as she had decided. 'Who can tell for sure?'

Far above and behind them, they heard their mother's summons. On Sundays or holidays she rang a little bell at the door, thus distinguishing the day from plain working days, when she beat with a spoon on a tin plate.

'There!' said Rob suddenly, grabbing Ella's arm. 'He's there!'

The boy had emerged as if the bell must have drawn away all who dwelt on the island. Rob, in his excitement, moved sharply, and a stone rolled from under his foot and went bounding over the rocks to the shore.

The boy stepped back, but his instinct betrayed him. He looked up sharply.

They stood, the two above, the one below, suspended, staring at one another.

Who was to speak first? Ella did not know. Though Rob had been so blustering and keen he now stood struck into total silence. Ella looked down at the boy, standing as still as she was, frowning, narrowing his eyes against the sun. Unable to prevent herself, she smiled. That was a mistake. It showed weakness and made him master. His scowl if anything deepened, and in a loud, challenging voice, he shouted out,

'Well?'

'Come away up,' said Ella.

'Come away down!' he answered.

In his mouth the words were different and sounded a little absurd. He was never from this side the Border, Ella told herself, in a disapproving way. However far might it be that he had come alone?

'We will meet you below,' she said with dignity. And to show him she knew almost everything there was to know, she added, 'You will wait for us in the cave.'

She turned to make the gentle descent her lofty tone of voice seemed to demand, walking the twenty yards or so with Rob muttering at her elbow, 'We'll lose him! He'll not stay for us!'

'Let him do different,' said Ella, 'if he cares to swim.'

He was waiting at the cave mouth. He was standing like a hero, one hand on his hip, one foot upon a suitable small boulder, in an arrogant, commanding fashion. There was that lift to his hair Ella had already noted with a kind of pleasure, and as she came near and saw him better, she half knew him already. She remembered her mother's words about a flash in the eye that was a princely thing, and she felt as if she were floating, as if the air about them hummed with magic.

She said at once, not waiting for him to speak,

'From Mr Alexander?'

She was glad she had startled him and, just as much, she admired his quick recovery.

'Mr Alexander is dead.'

She sighed. 'So it was told. But none in this place liking to believe it.'

'Nearly a year ago.'

'If so or if not – why should you come to live in the dry cave?'

'To look round,' he said.

'Why would you want to?'

'To see how the place is cared for.'

'Will you listen to the mannie!' muttered Rob, standing defensively a little behind Ella.

'The place is cared for,' Ella said; and the breath all but went out of her as she asked, 'What's it to you if it's cared for or no?'

He looked at her in a considering way. The scowl had left him, but there was still that flash in the eye.

'I don't know who you are or what your name is,' he said, 'but I can tell you who I am. I am William Hamilton Alexander's grandson. I am Clement Hamilton Alexander.'

'Aye,' said Ella. 'I believe it.'

'This place is mine,' he said. 'The island is mine and everything that's on it. The house is mine – and everything that's in it. My grandfather left it to me in his will. I am his heir!'

For a moment there seemed nothing to say, for surely it had all been said? He left nothing for Ella to question, since he had merely confirmed what she had almost certainly known – though how it could be so she could not begin to understand.

It was Rob who found the first words.

'Mr Alexander'd never have any grandson of his live in a cave!'

It sounded very funny, after young Alexander's dramatic pronouncement. Ella put her hand over her mouth and she saw that the boy quickly checked a grin. Rob had stepped forward to speak, and he had bunched up his fists as if prepared to hurl himself at the intruder and beat him to the ground. He looked as funny as he sounded, but the remark was quite a practical one. To come upon Mr Alexander's grandson dwelling alone in a cave, even if only for a short spell in summertime, was a total contradiction of the Alexander legend as Ella and Rob had learnt it.

'You havena made any answer!' shouted Rob. 'Mr Almighty!'

'Rob!' cried Ella, and slapped at his hand. 'That's no way to speak! It's rude and it's a thought blasphemous.'

But she was bursting with laughter as her excitement bubbled inside her, and then Clement Alexander laughed, too. The worst was suddenly over, the tension eased, the practical side of the business emerged like a monster from its lair.

'Mr Alexander had only the one son,' Ella said. 'He'd been wed but a wee while ... Then he died in a terrible accident.' She frowned. 'How can you be his grandson?'

'You know everything! He'd been wed, as you call it, the best part of a whole year. That's plenty of time, you know,' he said, in a rather condescending manner, 'for a man to beget a son, even though he may not live to see him born.'

Ella blinked at the Biblical word that he used so grandly.

'Well, now ...' she said, non-commitally.

'Don't you know that he came home with my mother to tell his father that he was to have a grandchild?'

'I did not know that,' she answered. With her new understanding she thought that her mother would have found this difficult to tell – not for the reason that people seemed hardly ever to speak of babies till they were safe born, but also because it would have hurt her at that time to know of the coming child. She found herself suddenly overcome by so much revelation, and knew that her face was red, she was blushing for the first time in her life ...

Some movement in the sky, birds flashing over, made Clement look upward.

'Better get inside,' he said. 'I don't want anyone more to find me. Things are bad enough as they are.'

The three of them went into the cave. It was always dry as bones, its silver sand soft like fine-milled flour, its walls bleached and pure. Above the entrance, sand martins came year after year to the same nest holes. The cave was no more than seven or eight feet from the cliff top, and because of the solid rock there the only planting ever undertaken was of small things that crept or mounded into neat cushions.

The signs of living within the cave were slight; sadly so, Ella thought. There was just a coat spread for sitting and presumably for sleeping, and there was a knapsack in which there must be food and a knife and a cup at the least. Then she saw there was a pile of rubbish that he had tried to burn, some packets and paper bags.

'Things are bad enough?' she repeated. 'What is bad?'

'I've not much food left, that's what's bad.'

'You must have brought a lot, you have been here a while already.'

'The boat boy came twice with food. He should have been again yesterday. I suppose someone's stopped him coming.'

'The boat boy? That is Hamish Macmillan and deserves his name to be called by. *When* has he come here?' she cried, outraged that she should have missed him.

'He rowed over when it was nearly dark.'

'He is the only son of his mother, and she a widow,' said Ella, sounding Biblical in her turn, 'He has little time to row hither and yon bringing food for such as you. And what of the money to buy it? Did you give him money?'

He looked uneasy, reddened a little. 'I'm short of money at the moment ... Anyway, I still don't know who you are. I don't know why I'm talking to you at all.'

'I am Ella Ross. And this is my brother, Robert. He is mostly called Rob. We are grandchildren, as much as you. We are the gardener's grandchildren. You'll have heard of our grandfather, no doubt, from your own.'

'I've heard of the gardener – of course I have.'

'He has a name, too,' she said, even sharper than she had been on Hamish's behalf. 'He is John Maitland.'

'I know that ...' He sat down suddenly on the spread coat and pulled his feet under him. 'What has been happening all these years? I think my grandfather meant to come back – I know he did.

'"Keep it as I would wish to find it," he said to our grandfather. And so he has done all these years. And so you will find it. It is Innis Gharaidh, the garden isle, Granda has made it that. And our father, who is now dead. And Rob and me. All of us have made it. It is as Mr Alexander would wish to find it.'

'Have you not seen it yourself?' Rob cried.

'Yes, I have. In the very early morning. I think,' Clement Alexander said, very slowly, 'it must be the most beautiful place on earth.'

'Then come home with us now.'

'No. I shall be chased after soon enough without anyone sending telegrams and that sort of thing.'

For the first time Ella thought about how he had come there, from a long way away, and only the last small lap of the journey with Hamish in his boat. He must indeed have come from England, as she had supposed from the different sound of him, and it was miles, hundreds of miles, Granda had said. She looked at him with admiration, forgiving him the arrogance which had made her rebuke him.

'Who'll chase after you?' asked Rob, his anger gone, dazzled as Ella was by the boy's prowess.

'Plenty will, perhaps. I should be at school. They'll have discovered long ago that I'm missing. I expect the hunt's on already.'

'How brave you are, Clement Alexander!' cried Ella. 'You have come so far!'

'Well, yes, it's a long way,' he said casually, as if well accustomed to such journeying. 'But there are trains, you know. One need only buy a ticket and take a train.'

She did not much like his manner now. He might be what he claimed to be, the new young laird of Innis Gharaidh – but he was in hiding, for reasons best known to himself, and what happened next to him depended on her and on Rob.

'The train took you no further than the loch head,' she reminded him.

'I got a steamer there. It might have been waiting just for me.'

'It was not,' said Ella. 'That was the supply boat.' She looked at him sternly. 'That would cost a pretty penny. You said you had no money.'

'I had money. It's gone. That's the way with money, you know – you spend it or you keep it. My grandfather used to slip me whole fivers – I had quite a hoard for a while. But when I really needed money I had to get hold of more.' He said rather sharply, as if accusing her rather then himself, 'If you must know, I stole from my mother. She came to school to tell me about my grandfather's will – that the island would be mine when I was twenty-one. They had only just heard from the lawyers – it takes a long time for such things to get settled. How could I wait till I'm twenty-one? It's *years*!'

He looked defiantly at Ella and Rob, who could hardly believe their ears – not that the island was his, but that he had stolen to come and see it. He must have been well aware of their shock, for his manner became determinedly jaunty.

'I shall stay where I am until the very last moment,' he said. 'I shall be thinking of some way to pay back my mother. When I pay it back it will be just as if it was never stolen.'

Ella did not reply directly to this, for she was too confused to know quite what he was talking about – perhaps he did not know himself. It was at this moment that Margaret rang the bell for at least the third time, and it was clear that the summons had better be answered.

'What food have you?' Ella asked.

'Some toffee ...'

94

'Only that?'

'Apples. Some lumps of sugar ... What will you be eating?'

'Don't tell him, Rob!' cried Ella, seeing him open his mouth to answer. She was not one to torment a starving man.

'We will bring what we can.' Seeing Rob looking hungry at the very thought of giving up his own victuals, Ella said sharply, 'Hold your tongue till I tell you let it go!'

She went out of the cave without looking back, and after kicking up the sand at the entry, Rob followed. As they went on their way, Ella heard Clement Alexander call after them, 'Don't be long!' She wondered was he more hungry or lonely ...

There was so much to think about that Ella hardly spoke as she sat at table. She slid a scone to her lap, then to her pocket. Then a second joined the first. Rob was not so handy – he dropped his first scone and was obliged to pick it up, rebuked by Margaret for his poor manners. Later, however, Ella knew that he had done better with a couple of bannocks. She became fascinated with the skill of the game and even managed to slip an egg among the rest – in its shell, but soft boiled, so she was bound to sit rather still to protect it. Cold meat, she thought, would not be impossible to deal with. The thought of the fugitive in the cave filled her with elation, but also with fear. No one could hide properly in a place from which there was no escape. He was threatened on all sides – it could not be much longer that the island dwellers kept themselves without a trip to the mainland. Or Miss Christabel might find time to come visiting – it was almost time for her do so so, since she had fallen into the way of Saturday calling every so often. And then there was Hamish, who had helped and then stayed away. Why should that be? This was two or three bothers rolled into one, but there was another that suddenly appeared to Ella and chilled her. Mr Alexander's grandson would want to know about the house that would one day be his, he would be anxious, surely, to see what was inside it ... And perhaps there was less than there ought to be – such as silver spoons and forks.

8

Now they began to learn about Mr Alexander. In secrecy and guilt they found themselves the possessors of knowledge far beyond any their grandfather could have guessed at. They took what food they could to Clement, and then sat in the dry cave for a bit to give him a little company and cheer him up. He did not seem, now, to be enjoying his situation, and Ella found herself unexpectedly impatient with him for having managed things so badly. Her first awe of his achievement had worn off. She had begun to worry about him, about how to get him indoors, about how to confess to these days of awful deceit ... But it was both extraordinary and enthralling to hear him talk of his grandfather.

'It took him years and years and *years* to find us – my mother and me. Did you know that?' As they solemnly shook their heads he said shortly, 'Well, how could you?' He frowned at them. 'Have you lived here *all your lives*?' He made it sound a very long time and seemed to suggest that they might not have tried hard enough. 'The world's a huge place. You must know that much. And he went round the world and back again. Grandfather, I mean. There are millions of Alexanders and he had to find just one, and he didn't even know where to start.'

'How could he, indeed,' said Ella.

'And it wasn't even as easy as that,' Clement cried, quite triumphant at the thought of all the problems. 'You see, my mother was not Mrs Alexander any longer – she was Mrs Tremayne by then, because she had married again. She had not been married in England, either, for she had met my step-father in Canada – her sister is there and that's where I was born ... You could never count all the lawyers mixed up in the business!'

In her mind's eye, primed by all that she had read of such matters, Ella saw the Laird, worn out by long searching, safe home at last – saw his daughter-in-law, Clement's mother, tenderly forgiving him for tragedy long ago.

'So, one day,' she said, 'he came to your door.' She smiled. 'It was a happy ending!'

Clement laughed. 'For two pins, she'd have sent him packing!'

'But she did not! She did not! It was a happy ending!'

His mother was a widow for a second time by then, he explained.

'A poor widow! Then she would have been glad of him!'

'Not poor at all. Rather rich. My grandfather was ill by the time he found us – in his head, I mean. It was only in the last month of his life that his mind cleared. And he was so old, so awfully old ... He only had a little bit of a cold – and then he died.'

'Granda should have been let know,' said Ella, sternly.

'Aye, he should have been let know,' Rob echoed her, sad and reproachful.

'But my grandfather had said the money must be sent and nothing changed until the lawyers settled about his will – I told you that sort of business takes a great time. If your grandfather had thought the money was coming from my mother he might have been too proud to take it.'

'He would,' said Ella, proud in her turn.

'It's a fact,' said Rob, nodding.

'When he knows about the will – then it'll be different. There'll be nothing for him to worry about again, my mother says. It won't be just wages any more, but a gift from a friend – any man will take a gift from an old friend.'

'There was never a word for him in all the years,' Ella insisted. 'Yon's no way for a friend to behave – no, nor any such gentleman as Mr Alexander.'

'I told you – he was old and a bit strange in the head until the last,' Clement said.

Now they were easier together. Soon Ella might find courage to tell him he could not stay for ever in the cave. For one thing, he was altogether too hungry; and from sharing their food she and Rob were growing hungry, too. Also, last night for the first time there had been some remarks made about the way the pair of them vanished after meals, sometimes staying just long enough for their grandfather to instruct them in the next task, sometimes forgetting even that.

'It's good there's been none crossing to the mainland these many days,' she told Clement now. 'But soon they must go. There'll be no more hiding then. It must be well known you had Hamish row you over.'

'Hamish would not tell. He swore it.'

'He had no need to swear, Clement Alexander. Any would trust him. But such things are always known!'

Mimicking her inflexions, he cried, 'I like fine the way you call me! Ma fu' name, no less!'

'It is a good name,' she said. 'Alexander, as you must well know, is a name to be honoured on Innis Gharaidh.' She thought best not to speak of the mainland, and before Rob could put in an awkward word she told him to go on home ahead of her. He went grumbling, but he went.

'I wouldn't let any sister order me about!' said Clement.

'You have made no answer.'

'Did you ask any question?'

'When will you give up hiding?'

'They'll come for me soon enough,' he said.

'Your mother?'

'My stepbrother. James. James Tremayne.'

'A stepbrother! That's an awful thing!'

In the stories, such people always pushed out the rightful heir and behaved in a very bad sort of way. Lizzie Best was

98

stepmother to Alister, and he seemed to love her dearly, but Ella was in a mood to think more of Cinderella's plight.

Again he mocked her – 'It's no awfu' thing at all!'

'Is it not? Could he not take the island from you?'

He laughed. 'Why should he? He's years older than me and just been made a doctor. He's very good at examinations. He'll be a good doctor. Besides – he's nothing to do with the Alexanders. It's just that my mother married his father.'

It somehow irked Ella that Clement clearly admired and liked James Tremayne. Perhaps, even, he longed for the time when his stepbrother would appear and take charge ... She went away in a mood of furious discontent.

The evening was very light and fine. She paused on her way, looking out over the water. There was a boat at anchor some way out. It was their own *Roìn*, and Sgarbh sat there fishing. There was nothing unusual in that, or in the other quiet boats dotted about the water. But when the fishing was done they would most likely move together and shout a word or two, or Sgarbh would go to the village to drink there. He would be asked about the lad who came off the steamer and had Hamish Macmillan row him to the island some days past ...

'Where have you been?' her mother asked, as Ella went indoors.

'Watching the fishing.' She told herself it was not what Rob called a true lie ...

Next day she was waiting nervously for Sgarbh to speak out. She had told Rob what she feared and they waited together for the blow to fall. Nothing happened. All was as usual. The day went by in work and three times the cave was visited, once by Ella, twice by Rob. Ella would have gone again but she was sure that Sgarbh had his eye on her. He knew something, she decided, and was biding his time. His manner was as usual – friendly in the presence of Margaret or of John Maitland; short, unpleasantly teasing, taunting even, when he spoke to either of the children alone. That evening, when Ella felt restless and fidgeted about, putting down her book, sighing, staring out of the window, she was sure he grinned as he watched her. He sat unravelling a mass of twine, teasing it out with infinite patience, winding it onto a spool. Margaret knitted, her father sat silently smoking his pipe. Rob played patience, never getting a game to a good conclusion and at last, in exasperation, sending the cards flying across the table and on to the floor.

'Pick up every one,' said his mother. 'No, Ella – let him do it for himself.'

'Read to us, Ella,' Granda said.

Ella fetched the latest book Miss Christabel had lent her, a very long one, and started at the beginning with the feeling that she would never get through it to the end. It was difficult to read, about London in the old days, full of strange words and stranger-mannered characters. But Granda liked it, nodding his head and saying, 'Aye. Aye, so it was!' and would not let Ella close the book. She read till she was hoarse.

They had come indoors early, for the fine weather had lost itself in high grey cloud that soon began to lower over the Sound. Ella thought of the cave which, however miraculously dry in itself, yet faced out generously to the weather. She woke in the night and the rain had come as threatened and fell, not fierce but steady. It might well continue for hours, for as it swept in from the west there was nothing to halt it save the far headland where the beam from the lighthouse shortened against the wall of weather. She thought how little the cave dweller had to keep him warm. If it were not that since her father's death she shared room and bed with her mother, she would have padded out through the wet to carry him more cover. Instead, she lay thinking about him. How had he endured to live so long alone and uncared for? What did he think about, in all that time, how pass from one hour to the next? She had lent him books, but she doubted that he had ever opened them. It struck her that he had a high determination that must be like his grandfather's. It would be a gift of doubtful solace for any who might love him; she had seen what bitter sadness Mr Alexander had caused her own grandfather by so cutting himself off... She could not sleep for listening to the rain, wondering how to act for the best, wishing she might wake her mother and confide in her – yet knowing she would never find the right words.

Then she thought of all the keys on the big bunch hanging by the kitchen door – the keys of the lonely house that was his house now. If she could be bold enough to take the keys she could open the house that was now Clement Alexander's house and let him indoors to shelter. Her mother had only recently completed one more frenzied cleaning of the place – as if, Ella thought now, awed, she had had some secret knowledge of the heir's arrival. It meant that the house was likely to remain undisturbed, save for the ritual opening and closing of the curtains and shutters, until someone came in search of him.

Ella hardly slept after thinking about all this, knowing how Sgarbh had been in the house, suspecting yet not knowing that he had not wasted his time there. Also she kept trying to imagine the other strangers, the newcomers who would arrive – Clement's stepbrother, Dr James Tremayne, perhaps Mrs Tremayne herself ... Ella recalled the dreadful story of Clement's father, of his body washed up on the shore. If his mother should come again to the island, what might happen to any one of them – what would she bring with her of ill fortune? Ella's imagination raced and darkened. Beside her, her own mother slept peacefully enough, but how must she feel when she came to know all that Ella knew now? Would she hate Clement for his mother, or love him for his father's sake? Ella longed for morning when at least she would be busy about work that had become tedious to her these last days.

And in the morning, the first thing she did was to make sure that the keys on their ring hung safe in their place.

To her great shock, the hook was empty.

Surprisingly and pleasingly, the rain was over by eight o'clock and a bright day followed. By afternoon they would be working outside, no doubt, but for the morning Granda had set Rob to sweeping and cleaning the smallest greenhouse, and Ella was helping Margaret at home.

'Take a bowl, Ella, and see can you pick a few strawberries

for dinner. The rain'll have beat them down – the slugs'll be at them if we're not.'

Ella took the bowl her mother handed her, and then chose a second. She ran to the patch and picked the wet strawberries fast, some for her mother, some for Clement. By that time Margaret was busy at the copper, so Ella put the one bowl down on the table and ran off again without speaking. She took the rest of the fruit to the cave and found Rob there already. He had a great collection of tiny crabs and prawns and had cooked them in a tin over a carefully hidden fire.

'I swept the greenhouse first,' Rob said at once, seeing Ella frown.

'As well you did. Two away's one too many.'

'Och, I'm only a minute away,' he said.

Brother and sister stood watching as Clement fell on the fish, pulling the pink flesh from the shells as fast as he could, and even crunching some of them up, he was in such haste. Then he pounced on the strawberries and scooped them up just as quickly.

'Best mind the slugs,' said Ella. 'Rob, get away back now, before Granda looks for you.'

She looked with concern at Clement. He had never seemed so ravenous. Also the signs of rough living were on him. His hair had already a grown and tousled look. Though he was browned by the sun and the sea, he still looked hollow-eyed and thin from his meagre diet. His clothes were rumpled and shabby. Ella found herself concerned for his health. He seemed a bit wheezy and sniffed a lot as if he had caught cold. She knew she must get him out of the cave. She frowned at him in a fussy, womanly way, half wishing he might be discovered and therefore, willing or not, be cared for.

'I am bound to say this, Clement Alexander. It is time and more that you came safe indoors.'

'I like it here.'

'When your father and my mother were bairns they played together on this very shore.'

'You told me that yesterday.'

'Maybe.'

'And the day before.'

'Aye. I did.'

'I know what you mean – that she would like to look after me.'

'She might,' said Ella, not wishing to commit her mother too far. But she could not help seeing this course a good deal easier to perform than her own wild ideas about stolen keys. 'She might well,' she added, deciding to go a step further.

'I'd be all right if that boy had kept his word.'

'He would never break it!'

'Then why hasn't he come with food, as he said he would?'

'He would have no money!' Ella cried. 'You said yourself you've none left.'

At the mention of it, of the money he had grabbed for his own purposes, Clement's face so twisted in distress that she feared he might cry. She saw indeed that he was defeated by his own wild behaviour, stealing, coming so far, living so hard. They had not spoken of the money since that first time. When she saw how greatly it filled his mind her whole purpose was to comfort him.

'You could live dry inside your own fine house,' she said. 'It has many treasures.' She paused, remembering Sgarbh. But then she remembered also Mrs Alexander's jewel box, which she had never been allowed to open. She rushed on, 'They are yours now. There would be ornaments and gewgaws you would give your mother to make up for the money.' She saw the idea sinking in and pushed her advantage. 'Why do you not wait comfortably there till your brother – your stepbrother – comes?'

'The place is locked up. I went there one night.'

'All doors have keys. I mind where they are kept.' She smiled at him. She was not sure that she had smiled at him since the very first day; she had been too busy looking after him and worrying. 'Will I bring them to you?'

He swung round, crying, '*Could* you?'

There was that princely flash again; it had been sadly absent lately.

'I could,' she said.

Before she was home Ella knew that she had been as impetuous and silly in her own way as Clement had been in his. Where would she ever find the keys now? Did Granda take them for safe-keeping overnight? Were they stolen by Sgarbh or left lying forgetfully by her mother? She remembered stories of keys stolen from sleeping gaolers – but such great bunches always dangled conveniently from the gaoler's belt. She saw them dangling in her imagination in much the same way as they dangled from their hook – and surely she had seen them there even yesterday? The trouble was that she was so used to them that she did not notice them any more particularly than she noticed what hung on the rest of the hooks there. Perhaps that morning Granda's old gardening hat, that usually hung next to the keys, had been hanging over them by mistake, completely hiding them.

She was stepping into the kitchen as she thought of this, and went straight to the far door and looked behind it. Sure enough, the keys hung as she had expected them to be hanging that morning.

In the room itself she heard her mother saying to Granda,

'When did you think of taking the boat across, father? We need flour, and that's by no means all. The steamer was in a few days ago. I have to write for knitting yarn and see that Maggie Ogilvie gets the letter off.'

There was a lot that needed doing, he said – the rain had been hard on many things: there would be trimming and staking.

'Then George Erskine must go.'

'No, no – I canna spare the man. The tide's right tomorrow and the next day – we've to mend that breach in the harbour wall.'

'We'll likely starve for bread, then,' said Margaret, short and vexed.

'You can take the boat yourself, lass – there's little to stop you that I can see. Haven't I said it's an easy tide? Short of noon's the best for going, and it'll let you home when you need. You can as well do your own messages as I can.'

'Oh aye, then I'll do that,' agreed Margaret. 'If I've time and to spare I'll visit Lizzie. It's a while since we spoke.'

Ella stood still beyond the door. She saw the colours of the story fading and try as she would she could not get breath enough to blow on them, as on a dying fire. She could see Rob in the scullery, washing his hands under the pump. She knew he had heard, too, for he looked round quickly. But Rob did not know what plans were afoot, or how the time for their fulfilment was shortening . . .

Granda was saying now, 'If you go to Lizzie, you could maybe take Rob and Ella.'

'I might . . . And now you speak of it, father, they'd be better for a day or two from work. You keep them at it as if they were full grown and twice as strong. It is summertime. They're aye running off, and that's a sign they're weary. They need to play a little. Ella's grown much lately – but Rob's still a bairn. Oh, this garden! This garden!'

Now Rob had come into the room, hot and red at hearing himself so described. His mother broke off, saying. 'Well, never mind . . . Come at once to the table, Robert! Canna you see we're all of us waiting on you?'

Ella muttered under her breath, as she took her place, 'He's not the last . . .' For Sgarbh had only just walked in.

By now both Rob and Ella had grown skilled at saving food for Clement. Fortunately the family had always been able to eat well enough, thanks to the Laird's money. It was Ella's job to take away the used plates into the kitchen and bring the pudding. No one seemed to notice that she took longer about it these days, scooping out any remaining potato, even slicing a bit of meat as she grew bolder, or spooning out some stew. For once she felt glad they had no dog, for it would have been robbed for Clement. The cat, indeed, was growing rather fretful, and Rob had to feed the poor creature secretly on collections of fish too small even for Clement's ravening appetite.

No doubt because of their mother's remarks, Granda said

he could do without the pair of them that afternoon as well as the next. At the first opportunity, they rushed off with their spoils to the cave. The sunshine had improved Clement's appearance, but he was coughing more than in the morning.

'Well?' he said to Ella instantly.

'I have not yet taken the key. A great bunch of keys makes an awfu' noise.'

'You only need one!'

'But I must take the one from a great many. They jostle and jangle like church bells,' she said, choosing words she had recently come upon. 'Don't stand there like a daftie, Rob! It's clear he must go into his own house. You can see that, I should hope?'

'It's the first you said of it ... What'll Granda say?'

'Never mind,' snapped Ella. 'It's no matter at all since he must know soon enough.'

'If you can't get the key –' Clement began.

'Whisht, you,' said Ella. 'Bide quiet one more night and then you'll see.'

'What do you expect me to do, then?'

'You must get yourself up by the house after noon the morrow. Mother and Rob are going to the mainland, but I shall be there to let you in.'

'You are to come too!' cried Rob.

'I am – but I am not.'

'I'd like fine to stay,' said Rob, wailing a little.

'You will go in the boat. I have my plans made and you'll not spoil them for me ... But a day from now, Clement Alexander, you'll be stepping across your own hearthstone!' She smiled in a triumphant manner. 'You'll be safe among all those things that you are heir to!'

Although she had not forgotten the matter of the silver, the grand words filled her with excitement. They were the words of a heroine – indeed, they were every syllable the words of a heroine in a fine tale Miss Christabel had brought with her on her last visit. The book had a blue cover with gold lettering, and Ella somehow felt that the words she spoke out so boldly were in gold, too. She had known from the moment that Granda spoke of an easy tide that an end was in sight – but they would make it as grand an ending as possible. She would not have Clement sneaking out of his cave to be taken alive. Rather, he should stand in the hall of his own fine dwelling, the new laird of Innis Gharaidh, like some chieftain standing for the clan to do him homage . . . Unaccountably, her eyes filled with tears. She could not see beyond that moment, any more than her own mother had seen what more might follow, when all those years ago she and Clement's father ran together along the sandy shore.

Next day they had their dinner sharp at noon, and it was a cold meal that it might be the easier cleared away.

'Leave the dishes drain, Ella,' Margaret said. 'Away now and brush your hair. And Rob, also. Waste no time about it.'

She was washing her hands as she spoke and then smoothing her own fine dark hair before the square of mirror hung above the sink. Then she took down her summer hat, a round straw, that as far as Ella was concerned she had possessed for ever. She anchored it carefully with two long hatpins through the big knot of hair at the back of her head. It was so firm and steady that the breeze on the water would not shift it.

Watching her mother Ella's heart began to thump uncomfortably. She was unused to disobeying.

'Ella! Wake up! Get your hair brushed. I'm already on my way, so no dawdling. Rob – come with me. You're to carry a jar of pickle I am taking for Lizzie . . . Are you dreaming, Ella Ross? The tide'll no wait for ever!'

Ella jumped, for she was indeed dreaming. She went upstairs and picked up a brush. From the window she watched her mother and Rob setting off, Rob hauling the great crock of pickle, Margaret herself carrying two vast shopping bags. Walking away in the opposite direction she saw her grandfather. Then she saw Sgarbh following after the old man. They carried between them the necessary tools for the afternoon's task, that the gentle tide made suitable, turning at the precisely right hour, not only for the work but to carry *Roin* to and from the mainland.

When she had seen them all out of sight, cold in the pit of her stomach and the small of her back, Ella dashed downstairs. The keys were on their hook. She reached up and seized the bunch, which did indeed jostle and jangle like church bells, even if rather distant ones. As she ran out of the house she heard her name, her mother calling on a long, long note. 'E—lla! E—lla!' She ran on, trying to close her ears. Her name came again, sharply now: '*Ella!*' Then Rob joined in, whistling and shouting. It was what she had said he should do, but for once she had not been absolutely certain of him, for he had hated going. She smiled slightly and still ran. In the noon of the summer day the birds were silent, though a gull or two sailed idly on a rising current of air, and a flight of terns flashed along the rocks. The calling after her ceased. As she reached the house and slipped into cover she knew that she had been abandoned – from the cliff top she would have seen the boat setting out across the channel, for as her mother had said, the tide would not wait.

She stood in shadow and looked around her, at the quiet house, at the sunlit garden island, seeing nothing, since she looked for one thing only. Then some slight movement caught her attention. Clement was waiting by the stone steps that led up to the front door. He had been lurking in a stretch of shadow, no doubt, but when he saw her he stepped forward. She would not forget how she ran to him and he held out his hand. She grabbed it, drawing him away from the exposed front of the house into the more secret clutter of sheds and outbuildings that lay about the back quarters – laundry, dairy, engine room with its snorting water pump. When finally she halted it was by the door to the passage that led into the pantries and the kitchen. They stood trying to get their breath back and Ella fumbled over the keys.

They had gone in silence, but now Clement spoke:

'There ought to be a book written about you,' he said.

She dropped the keys in her excitement, and they both groped for them – she was not accustomed to having things picked up that she had dropped. They banged into one another and laughed nervously, he rubbing his temples hard, though she knew she had butted him somewhere under the ear.

'I have it!' she cried at last, judging only by the size of it. She tried to fit the key but her fingers were shaking.

'There it goes,' he said, as the door opened.

Paralysed, she saw him shove the door wide, then stand back for her to enter first.

'What did you say, Ella?'

She shook her head.

She had in fact opened her mouth and the first word had come before she had bitten back the rest.

She had been going to say, 'It wasna locked!'

9

All this time Ella had been thinking only a little way ahead. She could do no more for she had never plotted until now. So far it had seemed easy, but now she saw with alarm how each small movement grew out of the last, how one thing led to half a dozen more, how the pattern changed, faded, grew threadbare. There was someone at work far cleverer than she was and her confusion was great as she saw how what had seemed a careful plan could be flicked aside and made useless by one movement from another quarter ... Her mind raced so painfully for a second or two that she feared she might start to cry.

Her eyes, in fact, did fill with tears, but blinking them away furiously, she grabbed Clement's hand, crying in a voice that broke and wobbled, 'Come away in till I show you!'

She drew him fast along the narrow dark passageway. Deep as a cave, the kitchen gaped in silence, the copper pots along its high shelves gleaming like stalactites where a shaft or two of light pierced the gloom. At the end of the passage was a door that swung, very quiet as they pushed through, sighing closed behind them. They were alongside the staircase then, and the hall with its pictures and cases of dead birds, its skin rugs on the fine floor so diligently polished over the years that it was like the surface of a lake, the rugs like rafts stilly floating. In a way the house had blossomed just as the garden had, for none came to tramp with dirty boots over the floors, and so the shine had grown all the while finer as the wood was fed with linseed and turpentine and beeswax and rubbed to perfection.

As with the hall floor and the stairs, so with the furniture. She led him from room to room. The sun was on the front of the house, and because of Margaret's dislike of blanking the windows with closed curtains, the light poured in, showing certainly a fading of carpet and hangings, but setting great rosy pools on mahogany and walnut, and striking against the sturdiness of oak that not even time could soften.

'Here is your dining-room,' she said. 'Here is your set of fine chairs.'

She offered him what was his own as if thrusting it into his hands, as if desperate to know that he accepted it.

He said nothing at all, looking over the place with eyes of amazement and wonder, frowning at one moment, smiling the next, touching, smoothing – only as he seemed likely to pull open the drawers of the sideboard where the polished silver should be lying, she drew him away, crying.

'Will I show you your drawing-room?'

Still he followed, still without a word. In the drawing-room the chairs with tapestry seats stood as they had stood for years, waiting to be drawn forward from the wall. Before the fireplace a deep sofa was set with many cushions, some with delicate embroidery, all smooth and undented. On the floor, the thick carpet seemed spread less to adorn than to muffle every footfall; here was the stillest quiet of all. It was many years since the big beautiful mirror above the hearth – brought, her mother had once told Ella, from a great house in France – had thrown back any new image. Now it held Clement and he stared back and very slightly nodded his head. To Ella he seemed already taller than when she had begun to lay his inheritance before him. He walked with his shoulders thrown back, and with clenched hands now – as if it were no longer necessary to touch, for everything had accepted his grasp.

Next to the dining-room was a little morning-room, where Mr Alexander had sat with his beautiful wife. Long ago as she had died, her memory was in this room. By the fireplace was her sewing-box. For once there was no one to tell Ella not to touch. She opened the box. Inside, the spools of coloured silks and cottons were neatly ranged, but in their case, with its pinked flannel leaves, the needles had rusted. There was one with a length of white thread in it, jabbed in crookedly among the rest. It was as if it had been hastily put down, before some piece of work was finished ... Perhaps as she rose to her feet in fright, knowing she must now take to her bed ... How strange that Lizzie Best must have been there that day. Lizzie might even have taken the needle and thread away and thrust it quickly and carelessly where it now remained ...

'My grandmother,' said Clement. They were the first words he had spoken. They came out hoarsely because of the cold settled on his chest, and because he had been so long silent; and because, surely, he was very much amazed and overcome.

'She was the beautiful Mrs Alexander,' Ella said. 'That is what Granda tells they all called her. The house was filled with treasures but none more beautiful than the Laird's beautiful wife.'

He nodded, half smiling. Then she led him upstairs. They stood by the high wide window that looked out, far beyond the Sound, where the spray burst interminably at the foot of the lighthouse, where the ocean spread for ever in the bright after-noon. Behind them, the length of the wall, was the clothes closet from which Margaret had plucked the black skirt and the lavender silk dress. Ella looked over her shoulder at the closet, and all the dresses and the coats and the cloaks hanging hidden there, seemed to her to shift very slightly, like a once fashionable crowd moving and murmuring at a long-forgotten gathering ...

They went from one bedroom to another, to the bathroom where in one corner a great bath stood on fat curled legs, a little raised above the floor, which was covered in black and white chequered linoleum. The taps of both bath and basin gleamed, and along under the windows were many cans, some bright polished copper or brass, some spotless white enamel; they would have been used to carry hot water to the bedrooms, to be poured into the bowls of white china decorated with

roses, with violets and with ivy leaves. Next door was the water
closet, its shining mahogany seat enclosing a bowl of blue and
white china – Ella wondered should she draw attention to such
a thing, and decided that she could not, in spite of thinking
it so elegant. Clement saved her embarrassment by finding it for
himself; he said nothing of the patterned china, a design of
pinks and nasturtiums, but closed the door discreetly.

The house was not so big as many such a house might be,
but neatly planned round the central staircase, with a flight
of back stairs running from the attics down to the kitchen. The
larger of the two attic bedrooms had been Lizzie's, Ella knew,
and the little one, almost filled by its bed, had been shared by
two young women from the mainland – Ailsa Dougal to cook,
Rosy Maclean to take care of the housework ...

Now the picture of his house and all inside it began to
spread itself, Ella saw, like light through Clement's imagination.
He sat down on the top stair of all and leaned against the
banister, and after a second's hesitation she sat beside him.

'When I live here always,' he said dreamily, 'I shall have a
great many guests. I shall have servants to care for me and for
everyone I invite here. I shall have a fine steam launch
waiting at anchor to carry us back and forth. The drawing-
room will be full of beautiful ladies in evening dress and
handsome gentlemen wearing white ties and kid gloves. There
will be banquets – huge roasted birds on silver dishes, with
their tail feathers stuck in. Peacocks, I think.'

'You'll go far to find a peacock,' said Ella.

'Well – swan, then, or perhaps eagle ... People will come
from far and wide to see my garden isle. I shall be Laird of
Innis Gharaidh. I shall be famous.'

'Who's to do all the garden work?'

'John Maitland – who else?'

Ella said, faltering, 'You canna have the house for your own
till you are twenty-one years of age. Granda is already an old
man.'

'Rob, then,' he said quickly.

'Or Hamish Macmillan. He's set to be a gardener. Though

Rob'll likely grow to be good at it – he has a douce hand with young plants, so Granda says.' Then she said, though she wished she would not, 'What plans have you for Rob's sister, if I may ask?'

'Ah!' he said.

He rose at once and ran down the stairs. She sat and watched him go, remembering how he had said there should be a book written, and written about her ... She thought also that she was the gardener's granddaughter and he was the old laird's grandson, and becoming more so with every moment that passed – she could find nothing in the two that would match once he came to his estate. 'Came to his estate' was a helpful-sounding phrase that was often used in books; but when it was lifted off its page it seemed to grow a colder meaning. Ella put her hands over her cheeks and thought about her mother and about Clement's father; long ago ...

She heard him moving about downstairs, coughing a bit, opening the door of the gun-room, whistling at what he found, everything clean and oiled and polished and neatly racked. The sound of him down there pleased her. She closed her eyes to listen better and almost drowsed, slipping into imaginings so wild she could not even halt their heady flight. The long frail trailing skirts of the beautiful Mrs Alexander seemed to float about her; she drifted down the stairs, her feet never touching the treads, her hand light on the banister rail; from the drawing-room the voices of guests were heard in elegant quiet conversation, an occasional light laugh breaking the murmur ...

She bumped awake as the sounds changed below. She heard Clement calling her name. Then the thudding open and shut of drawers and cupboards.

'Ella! Come here!'

She went down the stairs so fast that she had to jump the last three and flopped on her knees at the bottom.

Clement was standing in the dining-room by the sideboard, staring into the open drawers.

He said, frowning, 'Should they be empty? My grandfather said there was silver – spoons and things – with a crest ...'

She could not think how to reply for a moment. She stood a little back and craned slightly to see the emptiness of the felt-lined drawers.

'Has someone been using them?' he asked in an accusing voice.

She shook her head. Then she managed, 'I know who has them.'

'Oh –' He sounded relieved and smiled. 'That's all right, then.'

'I mean – I know who has stolen them.'

'Oh Ella – how? How?'

'It is Sgarbh took them,' she said.

'I don't know what you mean.'

'George Erskine. He is the man works with Granda in the garden. Rob named him Sgarbh.'

'What's *Sgarbh*?'

'It is the other word for cormorant. He is black in his looks and ugly in his ways. So it is a good name for him.'

'But if you knew – ?'

'He came to Innis Gharaidh when my father died. Because of the work. To do my father's work.'

'He's still here, Ella – but you *knew*!'

'For a matter of that,' she answered, her voice sharpening, 'we could have taken them for ourselves had we wished. Take what you need, Mr Alexander said. But we did not need silver spoons to our meat.'

'Of course you wouldn't take the silver – I know that. And my grandfather knew it, too, or he never would have told me where to look.'

'Thank you for your great trust,' she said.

'Oh, Ella, don't!' He hesitated as if he was not sure how to go on with this matter. 'But please,' he said at last, '*please* tell me why he is here if you know he's been stealing from my house.'

'Granda does not know.'

'Only you, then?'

'My mother.'

'Well, then ...'

'She – would like him to stay,' Ella said, looking at her hands.

'Do you know what he's done with the silver?'

She shook her head. 'But he plans to steal more. I am sure of that. The door – the door we came by had been unlocked already. You didna see that. He had taken the keys and opened the door and then put the keys back. Oh I see how it is!' she cried, suddenly and most painfully enlightened, 'He has known these past days that you have been on the island. It would have been as I thought – that he went ashore after fishing and was drinking there, and they asked did he know the lad brought to the island by Hamish Macmillan ... D'you not see? He has guessed and he has made his plans. He'll be away any time – for he knows my mother must know too by the time she comes home. She may speak to few, of choice, but there'll be many glad to speak to her now, for the sake of telling and finding out!'

'I wanted to give the silver to my mother,' Clement mumbled. 'Because of the money ...'

'We had best see what else is missing,' Ella said. She was shaking with misery and with sudden fright. What if Sgarbh came into the house now, sneaking up from the shore where he had been working, thinking to find the door open on an empty house. What might he do when he found them there before him? 'Come away upstairs,' she cried, feeling that the move would at least set a little distance between them and danger.

Now as they went back into the big bedroom where husband and wife all those years ago had slept happily in the great bed, she remembered the jewel case standing on the chest of drawers. It was shaped like a casket and stood on small feet, its lid and sides inlaid with a pattern of roses and delicate fern. Ella had the keys still heavy in her pocket, and she took them out and turned them one by one, seeking a key small enough to open the box. There were several that might do, and at last she handed the keys to Clement to let him choose and himself open the lid.

'When I was little,' she told him, as he picked over the keys, 'I was for ever wanting it open, but my mother would not so much as let me touch it.'

Clement stood with his hands either side of the casket.

'It's open now,' he said. 'The lock's broken.'

He put the lid back and they looked together into the box. It was stripped of all treasure, but in one corner, of little value and contemptuously ignored, was a thin silver chain, a sole survivor.

Clement took out the chain and held it in his hands. He might have been comforting it.

'I shall keep it, Ella. It's all there is left to me of my grandmother.'

She cried out, 'Oh what are we to do?'

'We must go to the police at once.'

'The police?'

'Isn't there a policeman in the village?'

'Losh, *no*! There's one comes from the town at times. And he will once in a while be rowed to the island to ask is all well.'

'But how often?'

'Twice a year, maybe.' Then she said in a sharp whisper, 'What's that?'

They stood utterly still, listening in a strained and frightened way – at least Ella was frightened, always fearful of Sgarbh, knowing more of him than Clement could know.

'There!'

Someone was below, moving gingerly – more cautious and lighter stepping than might have been expected of Sgarbh. Then someone spoke.

'Ella! Whisht! Whisht – are you there, Ella Ross?'

'Yon's Hamish Macmillan!' she cried; and ran fast to meet him, calling as she went, 'I am here! I am coming!'

There he stood at the foot of the stairs, looking bewildered and anxious, and completely awed at finding himself in that place at all.

'Ella!'

117

'I feared you'd be someone else, Hamish! How are you come here?'

'The door stood open.'

'I mean *why* – why are you come?'

'Ella, I never breathed a word of the laddie I rowed across and brought food for. But it is all about the village – and strange things said – very strange indeed. I wasna in school and I saw your mother go to the Macleans. She is there with Mistress Maclean telling every word she has learnt of it, I've not a doubt. I took Alister's boat, and never asked it of him, and came to speak with you and to warn you.'

'What'll you warn me of? What's *happening*, Hamish?'

Hamish was looking over her shoulder. Clement had come down the stairs behind her.

'Mon, I'd not know you!' Hamish said, 'You're half starved. I left you bonny enough – have you not been caring for him, Ella?'

'He has been in the dry cave – '

'Where else?' asked Clement.

'I thought for sure you'd be in safe with the Rosses by now.' He frowned and said to Ella, 'Is it not true, then, what they are saying? Is he no' the old laird's grandson?'

'How could they know that?'

'Then it's true?'

'It is,' said Ella solemnly. 'He has this reason and that, you ken, and does not care to be known. But this is his house and the island is his and he has but to wait till he comes to twenty-one years of age. Then he shall be laird of Innis Gharaidh.'

'That is more than they know on the mainland,' Hamish said, sounding pleased enough to be ahead of them. But he had come with a warning, as he had already said – to tell of a telegram arrived at the post, asking if Clement Hamilton Alexander had reached those parts, and requesting a reply to a given address. 'It was not a thing Maggie was like to keep to herself,' Hamish said. 'And your mother will be coming soon, Ella, to see what is the truth. My boat's below on the western beach, for I went first to the cave. But she'll be little more than a channel's width behind me.'

'The telegram,' Clement said. 'What was the name on the telegram?'

'It came through from the town, that is all I know.'

'How far, then? How far's that?'

'It is forty miles – or nearer fifty, maybe.'

'That will depend on the ferry,' Ella said.

'Aye. And on the tide,' agreed Hamish, nodding.

'My brother James must have sent it,' Clement said. 'Never mind how many miles, or the tide, or the ferry. He won't be long in coming, once he's sure I'm here.'

He sat down on the stairs and was silent, and neither Ella nor Hamish could have known whether he was feeling glad or sorry.

They had no time to consider it very deeply, for there sounded out over the island Margaret Ross's familiar summons, only louder and harsher than ever it had been heard before. She had reached home and stood at the door, beating with an iron spoon instead of a wooden, battering furiously on the old tin plate.

10

Returning with his mother to the island, Rob had had no easy time. When Ella ran indoors in answer to the spoon beaten on the plate, she saw him reduced to sullen tears. But she could be sure of him. He would never have given an inch. As things were now he had as well have spoken out and saved his own dignity; but he was not to know that.

'Ella!' Her mother's voice was more than sharp, it was harsh as Ella had never heard it. It was as if she herself had been changed by what she had heard, and changed, like the beating spoon, from wood to iron. Why was she so angry? Because she had been deceived by her own children? Ella knew it must be more than that, and struggling to understand, realized much. Her mother saw herself threatened, and the fear of it, the anticipation of coming wretchedness was in her voice. There came to Ella a fleeting vision of what Margaret had endured since the day she knew the silver was taken, and by whom. Her heart had defeated her conscience and that was bitter punishment for so upright a soul.

Ella had to stir herself to defiance, for otherwise she would have stood speechless, her own alarm and her mother's ringing through her head. She said, rude and harsh in her turn,

'Well?'

'*Ella!* Mind your manners!'

'What is it you want I should say?'

'A grand tale I've been hearing from Lizzie Best.'

'Have you heard a tale, mother? What would it be?'

'You know what tale! You have a young lad hid on the island these many days, and never a word spoken. Do you ken what he is calling himself?'

'Aye. I know.'

'You know? And you kept him hid?'

'It was *his wish*. Ask Rob if you dinna believe me.'

'No doubt at all – no doubt it was his wish! You are too stupid to see the matter of it!'

Ella chilled momentarily, hearing again the words *what he is calling himself*. But her mind cleared, for she knew altogether too much to take fright at what her mother seemed to suggest.

'I amna that stupid,' she said.

'Are you not? Tell me, then, what you think you know of him. You have made a great baby of yourself, Ella Ross, with your silly fairy tales and your high ideas – and I blame Miss Christabel! Tell me, then – go on, tell me.'

'He is Mr Alexander's grandson,' Ella said – and lost a little of the sound in the middle of the sentence.

'Did you not take him to be an impostor? Sent by those with longer heads to fool us all and take what is not his? Are you silly enough to believe every word spoken by a smooth tongue?'

Smooth tongue made Ella smile nervously, for it was an expression used in much of her reading to denote a fearful villain.

'Let me tell you, you foolish lass, that there is a telegram come, asking is he here? It'll be no wonder at all that the plot is discovered and the police are after him.'

'No,' said Ella, firm, though she did recall the stolen money. 'It will be his brother, he thinks – his stepbrother, that is – come after to find him. He ran from his school, mother,' she said, trying to soften her manner. 'All this way! He was in England and he came alone. Only think how it would be.'

She saw that this time she had well and truly caught her mother's attention. Margaret looked stunned.

'Brother? What brother?'

'Stepbrother,' said Rob, recovering a little now his sister was there to take the brunt of the business.

'What nonsense have you in mind now?'

'His mother is Mrs Tremayne, for she wed a second time. She has James Tremayne for her stepson, and Clement for her own.'

'Clement! The familiarity of it! If he is who you say he is – then you're a bold, forward lass and I am ashamed!'

Some black anger then closed Ella's mind and she gave up her attempt at kinder manners.

'Why,' she said, 'what name did you call his father by? It was never *Master William*?'

'Och, be silent, will you!'

'You never said how when they came here that awful time – it was to tell she would have a baby soon.'

'No – for till this day only Lizzie Best knew so much ... But she told no more. There was none of this second marrying ...' Margaret recovered her harshness, crying out angrily, 'Why do I talk to you of such matters? You'll mind you've played your part and now you'll stay quiet till things are set to rights. The telegram is answered. They'll likely be here for him by the morrow. And if it is a stepbrother who comes for him I'll be greatly astonished; as you might be, too, if you were any more than a silly bairn.'

Ella's own sudden anger was passed, she looked at her mother in misery. Margaret was pale as ashes except for one red spot that had appeared on her left cheekbone. Her eyes looked enormous, dark and threatened. She walked about the kitchen as though she must be on the move or let herself be struck down.

'Mother,' said Ella, 'oh mother, listen! It is true. Ask Rob. It is all true. He knows about the house – he knows what should be there – for his grandfather told him.'

Margaret was suddenly still. 'Where is he?'

'He is – he is with Hamish.'

'An' who's he not to mind his own affairs? So he is in it, too! Ah – I mind now Lizzie said it was Hamish rowed the lad across ... Why cannot your great friend, Miss Christabel Galbraith keep Hamish safe at his lessons?'

'He knew what Lizzie would tell – and came to bring a warning.'

'I have not set eyes on Hamish Macmillan. There's no sign of a boat. You are lying to me, Ella!'

'Then how would I know of the telegram? Hamish was here before you were back. His boat's below in the west bay.'

Margaret was still a second.

'Fetch Granda, Rob,' she said then. 'Get Granda here.'

He went, glad to escape, speechless and frightened.

'Now, Ella,' said her mother, 'where are these two bold laddies? If you're not to fetch them here – then I will.'

'They are in the house,' said Ella – and hunched her shoulders a little, as if against a rising storm.

'In the house? In the *house*? You let them in ...?'

'Mother – oh mother, please! I have to tell you. The door was open for us! The door had been unlocked ... Mother, he is truly, truly the only grandson of Mr Alexander. He will be laird of Innis Gharaidh when he comes to his twenty-first birthday! I told you – I told you he knows what should be in the house. It was his grandfather told him! But he canna hope to find what is no longer there!'

Margaret dragged at a chair and sat down, leaning on the table, her face turned from Ella.

'The silver ...'

'Aye, the silver – the fine silver forks and spoons from the dining-room. And the jewel box in the big bedroom that you never let me see inside ... Oh mother, I am sorry for it!'

'Ella, Ella – could you not have bided a while? Maybe it could all be got back.'

Now Ella remembered other things she had admired about the house – things she had surely not seen that afternoon. The row of miniatures in their black and gold frames, hanging beside the great fireplace in the drawing-room; the enamel boxes delicately decorated with wreaths of flowers and mottoes, or with tiny pastoral scenes, all shapes and sizes, and all ranged prettily on a small table in the morning-room ... And there had been a case of fans, spread to show their ivory sticks and painted shepherds and shepherdesses picked out with gold. If she could remember so much, what more might there have been, easily removed, that she could not recall, that she had perhaps never seen?

'What will Granda say?' she cried in misery.

'It'll maybe kill him. He has lived all these years of his life for the honour of handing back what was left in his care. Oh Ella – what have you done to us all?'

Ella trembled and bit her lip, but it was not because she felt herself in any way to blame – how could she be? What made her tremble was what she had known at the back of her mind ever since she heard the tale of Mr Alexander and his son – that only between the covers of a book may a story be told just so, worked out in chosen words to a pleasing conclusion. Truth could only be truth – and if the end of the tale was to be a sad one, then sad it must be.

'He must go now,' her mother was saying, though only to herself, as if repeating something she had long known but kept inside her.

She meant Sgarbh . . .

Down on the shore, where Sgarbh was working with Granda, Rob would by now be blurting out something at least to bring the old man fast indoors. Then what would Sgarbh do? Would he go at once, or would he come indoors to brazen it out? Or might he, drawn by some as yet ungathered prize, take the risk of going to the house he had left purposely unlocked? She thought he would do that, for greed and daring, which anyone would expect of him, had made him dally already longer than he need. He could have gone days ago, when he first knew there was a stranger on the island. Yet he surely could not have known of the telegram, with its threat of discovery, for then indeed he would have gone. He had enemies on the mainland – maybe they had kept the latest news to themselves. But what he did not know, he was surely learning now from Rob. Her mother would have brought *Roin* in to the nearer beach, not the harbour where the men were working, there would have been no chance to flash any message or warning.

Then she remembered her mother's fierce summons sounding

out, and wondered that Granda and Sgarbh had not come to answer it. Perhaps Granda had said to Sgarbh, 'Go and find what she wants.' Or Sgarbh himself, alert to danger as he must surely be, had said himself, 'Will I go and find what she wants?'

Margaret was sitting utterly still, her face in her hands. Ella left her and went out of the cottage, thinking of Clement and Hamish in the house, a poor match for such a man as Sgarbh. She began at once to run fast to warn them.

Then she saw that Sgarbh was indeed ahead of her, skirting the far wall, moving steadily and strongly and with speed, as a cormorant flies dark and strong and outstretched, along the line of the water.

The island seemed to Ella at this moment to be empty of hope. There was no one to call to for help save Granda, and how would he stand any firmer against Sgarbh than two young lads? There was Rob, too small to be helpful; there was Margaret. Of this poor muster she was no doubt the strongest, but there was no will in her, clearly enough, to move against Sgarbh. Checking her own flight towards the house, Ella stood still and watched Sgarbh. He was making for the door he knew to be open. He would not know, since Rob had not known it, that the house was no longer empty. She stood uncertain, torn between two possible courses: she might follow Sgarbh in, or she might go at once to warn the two boys. She thought it best to warn them, for in any case she was too frightened of Sgarbh to think of challenging him.

Ella ran round to the front of the house. She began moving from window to window, picking her way among the careful shrubs, in many places close clipped against the walls, so that they snatched and grabbed as she struggled to get near the glass to see if the boys were inside. She saw them nowhere; the dining-room, the drawing-room, the little neat morning-room were all empty. She would be obliged to bang on the big door, and this she did not at all want to do, since it must also attract the attention of Sgarbh. She had some vague idea of bringing the boys out of the house and then locking

Sgarbh inside. That he could very easily open a window and climb out did not at this moment occur to her. If her mind had not been so confused by what was real and what was not, she might have remembered that the keys themselves were now somewhere inside the house; for she had handed them to Clement in order to open, as they had supposed, his grandmother's jewel box.

By now growing frantic, she stepped back a little and looked up at the bedroom windows one by one, running furtively round the house in a hopeful yet hopeless fashion. In such predicaments, she recalled, stones were thrown up to patter on the glass with wonderful effect – for sashes were then lifted, casements thrust open, and always the longed-for face appeared to gaze down in query . . . She picked up a handful of gravel and hurled it, but it all pattered back, scattering itself over her head and even dropping back into her sleeve.

All this seemed to take an immeasurable time. She had been running round the house for ever. She heard herself moaning very quietly and knew she might break into sobs. Such circumstances as this, expertly told in many a tale, were outside her capabilities. If only Granda would appear – strong and striding as he had been when she first became aware of him . . . The childish fruitlessness of such longing brought her to her senses a little. She thought of him with misery. Who could say that he was not at this moment gasping for breath from the shock of what. Rob had run to tell him. Desperate, her eyes now ready to gush with tears, she ran to the main door, prepared to do more than merely knock – she would pull on the great bell and hear its clangour sound all through the house, all about the island, across the channel to the mainland.

The door, tough oak, magnificently weathered by the salt airs and the sun of decades, had also, like any other door, its keyhole. Spying through keyholes was the very height and horror of deceitful behaviour – even in this extremity Ella hesitated to slide back the little shutter that closed the keyhole. But there seemed nothing else for it, and she fumbled the shutter and set her eye against the hole.

The picture presented was amazing. Perhaps because the hole was small she had expected the interior to be presented to her in miniature. But she saw through the space of an inch and a half everything she would have seen with both her eyes had she been standing on the inside of the door. There was the wide hall, there its polished floor, the rugs that had once belonged to living animals, the paintings on the walls, the cases of stuffed birds. The sun was slanting pleasantly from the window on the stairs.

Of the boys there was still no sign, but immediately she heard them talking. The conversation was full of enthusiastic exclamations that she could not quite interpret. Then she heard Hamish say, 'No – that's a twelve-bore. It has a great fine kick to it. You dinna handle it right!'

So they were in the gun-room. They would never hear a gentle knocking, they were too much occupied. If she banged and thumped she might as well pull the bell.

Unwilling to take her eye from the keyhole, Ella groped about for the bell pull. It was a twisted iron rod attached to a bell just inside the door. There was an iron ring at the bottom and at last she found it. Her hand rested a moment more. The thought of the noise frightened her. Then she tugged violently.

As the bell pealed out, loud out of all proportion to its size, Ella's eye at the keyhole saw the picture change.

The stream of sunlight was broken. Sgarbh stepped through it and against it from the back of the house and came forward into the hall. He checked instantly as the noise struck him, standing stock still and looking sharply, even wildly round him, taken totally by surprise, and not knowing at all where best to turn.

At the same instant, the two boys ran out of the gun-room to the right of the hall. They looked as alarmed as Sgarbh himself. Of the three, Clement managed to appear the calmest. But that might have been because he was carrying a gun.

Ella knew perfectly well that the gun would not be loaded.

It had stood for years, neat and cared for and unused. Yet the sight of it, awkwardly held, filled her with terror. She thumped with her fists on the door, calling them by name, shouting out to them while she dared not take her eye from the keyhole, screaming 'Put it down! Put it down!'

She heard Clement cry out, 'Is it him?' and knew that Hamish answered as he came towards the door, thinking no doubt he had only to shoot a bolt or two to let her in.

Sgarbh moved faster than Hamish. As Clement stepped nervously forward, Sgarbh grabbed at the gun, broke it and tossed it away, then butted Hamish so hard to one side that he reeled backward and collapsed on the settle. Then Sgarbh was at the door and tugging at the handle. It must seem now his surest way out of the house, for now the boys were between him and the way he had entered. What he knew no more than Hamish had known, was that this was always the way Margaret came and went, not bolting on the inside, but locking behind her.

As Sgarbh grabbed the handle and shook the door, the rough stuff of his jacket was pressed against the keyhole, blanking out Ella's view and making her shrink back as if he might strike her. Then the keyhole cleared and she was watching again, seeing him swing across towards the dining-room, his only easy exit. As he went, he scooped up the fallen gun, hurling it almost casually at the two boys as they attempted to follow. There was a yelp from one of them, but Ella could not stay to see which. She was running wildly to the dining-room window, mad with excitement and terror, barely knowing what she was doing, what intending, grabbing at the window frame and hanging on fiercely – as if she would prevent his flinging up the sash.

Seeing her, he went instantly to the small side window and she stumbled through the bushes, believing herself strong enough to head him off. But she had forgotten the first thing about glass. She heard him shout out from inside,

'Mind away, now! Stand back, you silly lass!'

And she did step back, for his elbow was on the pane and the glass splintered easily, shattering and showering in all directions.

But Ella could not quite let go, she was wild to hold him, to keep him, to have him pay for his sins, every one of them. As he reached the ground, she threw herself against him, hanging on to his sleeve, twisting it fiercely between her fingers, while with her free hand she hammered at his chest, crying all the time, 'Wait, now! Wait, will you!' and expecting every instant to see the boys running to her help, not knowing that she was dealing in seconds and split seconds ...

He put his hands on her shoulders, shoving her, so that her head was back and she was staring up into his face. She gritted her teeth, expecting to be flung hard away from him into the rough thorny bushes.

Then as if touched by some pale ray of light, his face changed and he hesitated, looking down at her. Even in so strange a moment, when all that was known and real seemed vanishing into air, some part of her knew that she was seeing what she had never seen before. She was seeing what her mother had seen — a harsh, hard face blurred by tenderness, the dark piercing eyes softened, almost as if by tears. It was for this that her mother had sacrificed even the honour of Mr Alexander's house.

'Margaret ...' he said.

'Ella,' she said. 'I'm Ella.'

Then immediately he was his own self, all feeling shut away, a black scowl contorting his face. He shoved her, then, as she had been expecting — and ran instantly, fast and certain across the grass to the head of the cliff ...

Clement was the one who had been caught by the gun. He was holding the injured foot and hopping about with the pain. But Hamish was out through the window almost as soon as Sgarbh and starting after him. Ella saw her mother standing near the head of the path that ran down gently to the small western bay where Hamish had beached Alister Maclean's boat. She was beckoning and calling.

Ella caught Hamish's sleeve and hung on.

'Take off your hand from me!' Hamish shouted.

'Wait now, Hamish Macmillan! You canna stop him! You're

not the half strong enough. There's none here can stop Sgarbh flying across the water!'

He struggled and fought with her, crying out that she must be crazy. Because of the tussle they had, Ella did not see Sgarbh go, but by the time she released Hamish only Margaret stood by the path, looking downward.

'Yon's Alister's boat! He'll take Alister's boat!' Hamish was almost sobbing with rage. 'You daft thing – how'll I tell Alister I lost his boat for him?'

'Whisht,' said Ella, tired and shaking.

He dashed past her and went scrambling down to the shore. She did not stop to see how Clement was doing, but went rather slowly over the grass and then stood by her mother, almost leaning against her, saying nothing, watching Sgarbh already pulling away strong and dark across the quiet water, headed not for the village but round the headland to a more distant shore. The tide was right, now, for him, and he would make his landfall in an hour or two. The sun was behind him. They saw him raise his arm. Margaret answered the farewell, standing a long while slowly, slowly waving. Had he spoken to her as he bounded by? Paused to touch her hand? Or had his true farewell been that strange moment when he looked into Ella's face and saw her mother in it, and spoke her name? Ella would never know, she would never be able to speak of him, nor would Margaret. Steadily light and distance removed the boat from sight. Nothing remained to be saluted but the empty Sound and the open sea, the islands far ahead, their mountains received into mist, with eastward the loch running between narrowing shores, the distance land-held and unknowable.

What Rob had told his grandfather, gabbling and blurting and
falling over his words, had indeed been enough to cause John
Maitland to stagger a little. He had put out his hand and stood
resting against the first rock he came to, breathing very deeply
and stooping forward; as if, Rob told Ella later, he might
fold right up and fall upon the sand. But he righted himself,
and when he said, 'Where is he?' there was only joy in his
voice.

So he and Rob had gone up the path together, walking
slowly for safety's sake. Both forgot Sgarbh – which Rob was
ashamed to recall later ...

Margaret was saying to Ella then, speaking for the first time,
'We must find what has happened to Granda. They should be
here by now.'

In the same low voice, Ella answered her.

'They are here,' she said.

Margaret moved at once and went swiftly forward, taking
her father's hand and saying, 'It is a strange tale – a strange
tale – but I think it after all to be a true one.' She had
recovered her strength for his sake, and she spoke softly and
slowly, as if to make him understand. 'They are telling me it
is the laird's grandson, my dear.'

'Aye. So I hear it from Rob.' He smiled, patted her hand in
his turn, saying as he did so, 'I have it from my own grandson.
It is a strange thing, forebye, when the generations change.'

Clement was still standing on one foot, rubbing his instep where the hurled gun had struck him. As Ella watched her grandfather advance towards his young Alexander, she could have wished Clement might look a shade more dignified, less like a boy who has been hurt and is making the most of it.

When he saw the old man approaching, however, Clement stood properly upright on his own doorstep. Ella remembered how he had stood when they first found him in the cave, heroic and commanding; and she thought how she had seen him in her imagination, receiving the acclaim of clansmen come from far and wide ...

It was quite different now. He limped forward, and though with some dignity he held out his hand, Granda clasped it at once in both his own. So Clement added his other hand and what resulted was in a way an embrace.

'I am John Maitland,' she heard Granda saying. 'I was your grandfather's gardener, and he left all of this place in my care when he went seeking your mother. You have his features but your grandmother's fair colour. I would know you anywhere.'

'I would know you, also,' Clement answered; and in its way it was a true statement, as well as a tribute.

'"Keep it as we both would wish," he said when he went away ... I see by your coming that he is now dead. But you will find house and garden as he would wish you to.'

'Thank you,' said Clement. 'I am sure of it.'

Ella saw that Granda was upset by the meeting, knowing that the old laird would never come again, and saddened that there had come no word from him before the end. Margaret, too, saw that her father had tears in his eyes, and that his hands trembled. Still with that effort of will, shaking from her what must surely have been despair, she went to Clement and greeted him in her turn. Then she spoke clearly and bravely of his mother – and how at this time she must be worrying and wondering; and how he had best come indoors now, for she could see he had a bad cold on him, not to mention his foot needing bathing and bandaging. He should have the room, she told him, where his own father had often slept at about his age ...

Ella listened to the brave words and loved her mother as she had not done since the unthinking times when she was only six or seven years old. Nothing was said to spoil this moment for Granda. There was no talk of what was lost, nor any mention yet of the man who had gone, most likely for ever, as surely as if, like Mr Alexander, he had died.

Then she saw that Clement had in some way moved on. He was still a lad with a cold on his chest and a bruised foot, and his clothes were creased and shabby-looking. But in the assumption of his dignity as heir to Innis Gharaidh, that had come to him with John Maitland's greeting, he had cast off lesser business. It would no longer matter to him that he had in fact stolen as surely as Sgarbh had stolen – such petty concerns were swallowed in the dignity of his acknowledged situation . . . Much of this ran in Ella's mind and she found it uncomfortable. There was more that she must think about, but she would not let it in yet – she would keep it far at the back of her mind for as long as she was able.

They all began to shift towards the cottage, urged on by Margaret. Fussing over Clement had helped her to grow easier in manner – glad of a distraction from her own sorrows, perhaps finding in him something to remind her of his father. She bent herself towards caring for the boy, bundling him off to bed, sending Ella for more blankets, setting broth to heat, seeking in her store cupboard for what might ease his cold . . .

Ella went outside. Rob and Hamish were there, Hamish kicking miserably at a stone, sick with the knowledge of what he must tell Alister Maclean about his boat – borrowed in such haste that for once its owner's permission had been quite overlooked.

'Is the young laird made warm and comfy?' he asked rudely, when Ella appeared.

'You might think she was his mother,' said Ella, which was one way to answer.

'You might. And you might not,' said Hamish.

'You would not,' said Rob, growling it.

Ella turned away quickly from the two boys, who seemed to

see too much, and ran off without anywhere to go, still trying to busy her thoughts, building a dam against a threatening flood.

But the dam was already breached before it had been properly built and made firm. The thoughts, the realizations that Ella could no longer check, rushed and tumbled into her mind. She heard again words that had been spoken amid all the kindness and the welcoming, words that she knew she must listen to again and again, that she would, indeed, be expected to use herself. What was happening to her now was what had happened to her mother when the excuse of childhood no longer held her and Clement's father in the happy bond of friendship ... *Sir*, Granda had called his master's grandson; *Maitland*, the boy had called Granda in return ... But what of the tales Granda had told of Mr Alexander working with him, spit for spit, as they made the garden together? What of the friendship that had made them equals in their own world?

Then Granda's tales began to merge with those she had all but drowned herself in, ever since Miss Christabel came visiting, all that time ago. Some layer of wicked concealment was suddenly peeled away. The fairy tale ended for Ella then, and the truth she had once just contrived to see began stealthily, but ever more speedily, to possess her imagination. Again she knew her affinity with her mother. She, too, seemed to stand as Margaret had stood, waving a farewell ... She thought she would never be able to speak to Clement again.

It took two days more for newcomers to arrive, steaming prettily down the loch to drop anchor off shore. Clement's mother, with his stepbrother, James Tremayne, were rowed ashore. Granda went alone to meet them, no longer easy in manner, since by now he had learnt too much of what had been lost from the house. He escorted them to the cottage, and there followed almost more anger than emotion in the reunion of mother and son. Handsome James Tremayne laughed as he pronounced that young Clement Alexander needed a good hiding, but his mother was a great deal cooler. She complained that he had behaved like a spoilt child, that he had all but worried her into a sick bed; and she was not at all pleased that he had, as she put it, blatantly robbed her.

'Fetch him at once, James,' she had cried.

'He's no altogether himself –' Margaret began.

'He knows what is due to his mother, I hope. Fetch him, James.'

If James had not winked at Ella as he leapt up the stairs as ordered, she would have felt like shrinking away into hiding.

Ella had thought so much of Clement's mother – of the terrible disaster of her first husband's death, of her loneliness, of how she had now to endure a second widowhood – her worry and her fears when Clement ran away. But it was all quite different. She was altogether unlike Ella's imaginings. Whatever she had been in girlhood, however sweet, however shrinking, Mrs Tremayne had by now a manner easy and commanding. She gave no sign that she so much as remembered her previous visit to the island, still less that she was in any way moved at being there now. Her hair was beautifully dressed, her complexion barely flawed. When she peeled off her gloves as she waited for Clement to get respectably dressed to greet her, her hands, small and smooth, moved in a graceful almost rhythmic manner, the nails a perfect oval and buffed to a delicate sheen – the sight made Ella put her own hands behind her back. Over the whole figure of Mrs Tremayne, from her pretty straw hat to her feet in their fine soft shoes, and her dress which was neither too grand nor too plain, too warm or too flimsy, was a gloss that Ella needed no telling to recognize as the gloss of wealth.

But as the time moved on to viewing the house and garden, to explanations and to humble regrets, Mrs Tremayne disgraced herself even more in Ella's eyes – for she showed a complete indifference to what was missing from the house. That Clement should be generous and dismissive was good – but it was what she would have expected of him. He was not of age, it was for his guardians to be angry for him, probably to set about the pursuit and recovery of what had been stolen. Ella was not ready to accept any generosity on Mrs Tremayne's part. It was possible to think that she was comforting John Maitland by treating the matter as not worth a thought; or that Clement had told her of Sgarbh and of Margaret ... But to Ella it could only seem that all Granda's care, his toiling over the years, his feeling of being dishonoured when the thefts were disclosed to him, his proud acceptance of responsibility, had been reduced to so many grains of dust to be lightly blown away. She saw him, undeniably aged and shaken by what had occurred, coolly assured that it was a matter of no importance.

'My father-in-law would not wish you to blame yourself in any way whatever, Maitland. Such things occur in life and must be accepted. The house is full of treasure as it is.'

'I'd have liked fine to explain matters to the laird, ma'am.'

'Alas – that is sadly not possible. But he would certainly expect you to put the matter out of your mind.'

Then he said, unable to keep the reproach entirely to himself, 'I regret I had no word of him all the years.'

'Try to understand that for a long while he was by no means in his right mind.' She held up her hand at his glance of horror and alarm. 'Now, my dear good fellow, I am not saying he was mad! But he had had a terrible time seeking us out. He was worn out – in mind as well as body. It was only in the last weeks that his brain cleared and he was altogether himself again. It was only then that he sent for his lawyers and made his will afresh, that there might be no doubt about his intentions.' She smiled, tolerantly, as to a child who cannot quite understand. 'And he did not forget you, you see. You are safe here and need have no worries. The will takes care of you and of all your family – and there will be enough for you to employ some help in this great place.' She smiled again, but now distantly, ready to conclude and have done. 'And my son, who says this must be his home – and though he is only a boy, he does know his mind – he, too, has promised that you shall want for nothing.'

Was it the wealth that made her seem so aloof, or had her heart been so brutally broken all those years ago that it stayed scarred for ever? Such tales were told ... But Ella thrust the thought from her, no longer willing to be snared by tales.

The guests stayed on. The launch remained in the bay. All through the summer days the house stood open, and at night, in the warm darkness, light streamed from the open windows bringing with it the jangling sound of the piano, long out of tune, yet strangely plaintive. Clement was not sent to finish off the school term. He had James to thank for that, the young doctor solemnly pronouncing that the boy would be best where he was, making a complete recovery before departing in the autumn. Lizzie Best came to the house to look after the visitors with Margaret's help, and often Miss Christabel Galbraith was there, too. James Tremayne had discovered her. He had brought her, so he said, to keep Clement's wits in order until the next term.

Ella could have shared these lessons, as Rob suddenly agreed to, as James urged, as Miss Christabel begged. But she shrugged the idea away. If Clement had asked her – would she have given in? She did not know. And he gave no sign that he noticed her silent withdrawal, or asked her why it was so. He seemed content to accept Rob as a willing slave, and to exclude her from their doings. Ella watched her brother often, tagging cheerfully along behind Clement, carrying his fishing tackle, or the bread and cheese Lizzie had given them to keep their appetites happy as they sat on the shore or rowed out across the Sound. Ella despised Rob and she envied him. She longed for the days when they went without half their dinner for the sake of carrying it to Clement. Why was that so different? Ella could not tell.

During these lonely late summer days, Ella clung close by her grandfather, wanting to comfort him, not sure that he knew he needed it, trying to do enough work for three – for herself, for Rob who was forever truant and never rebuked since he was Clement's companion; and for Sgarbh who was gone and would not return. She worked so hard that she grew taller, and because she was taller grew thin, and grew older in her mind and her imagining and could not decide what she wanted most. Innis Gharaidh was at its best, the roses full and trailing, bursting with scent; the small cliff plantings of bright pinks and gentians hanging like patterned china on their rocky shelves.

Then one day the launch that had sometimes carried them on jaunts up the coast, or out beyond the lighthouse to the puffin places and the seals' grounds, got up steam for a longer journey. Mrs Tremayne was rowed aboard, and as the launch moved off stood waving briefly to those who remained on shore, then moved away to settle herself in the shade. Then in the house only the brothers were left. Lizzie went home in her turn, and Margaret cared for James and Clement. But Miss Christabel was still there almost daily. Ella thought this strange, for the school term was long, long over. Margaret said it was a disgrace, and as much as she could stayed about the house till Miss Christabel went home, with James Tremayne for boatman.

Ella was friends with James in a shy and awkward fashion, and then after a while more easily. He was gentle and kind and funny, and seemed to like talking to her and trying to make her laugh. He seemed puzzled by her and even anxious. He liked to sit on the cliffs overlooking the mainland and call her to sit by him.

Then he would begin an increasingly familiar game.

'Who lives in the last little house on the top of the hill?'

'Mistress Euan Macmillan, that is aunt to Hamish, and her husband, Rory, and their children, Angus and Annie and Morag.'

'And whose croft is that, way out in the far fields? Is that where Roderick and Gavin somebody-or-other live with their old father?'

'No, *no*! Did I not tell you last time and the time before? It is Davy and Tom Ross who live there, but –'

And then he would take her up, 'But no relation in the world, y'ken!'

That made Ella laugh, which was not a bad thing. She waited for his next question.

'What's that building, Ella, that stands in the centre of the village?'

'Is it the one with the wee belfry?'

'It is. And the bell silent, forebye.'

'It is the school!' she would cry, her hand over her mouth at his attempts at sounding as if he had lived long in these parts and knew the speech.

'Who lives,' then asked James Tremayne, 'in the house next the school?'

'You know fine who lives there!'

'Miss Christabel Galbraith.'

It took three or four occasions of this kind to make Ella suddenly cry out, 'I see! Oh I see!'

'And a long, long time you've taken to open your eyes. But don't tell anyone else. Miss Christabel has no idea – I think – that I intend to marry her.'

For a second all the glory rushed back for Ella – it was true, then! Such things could happen!

'She'll maybe no have you, Dr James!'

'Ella, you see that she does ... Now shall I tell you all my plans,' he said one day, 'that no one else in the world knows save my brother?'

She nodded, watching his face, a keen face, not too handsome, honest, true – so right, so right for beautiful Miss Christabel. He put his arm round her and spoke very confidentially. He told her how Clement would be bound to finish his education – back to school, on to the university, as his father had done before him, and from this very place.

'But I shall remain, Ella, to keep the house warm for him. And I shall work here. There is no doctor, they tell me, for fifteen miles at the least, and he's a very old man with his horse mostly lame in the shafts. Those days when it is stormy and I am bound to stay ashore, I think Lizzie Best will see I have a bed and supper. And I shall never let beautiful Miss Christabel rest – and you're not to, either – until she agrees to be my wife. Then we'll have a great fine wedding, and there shall be ten bridesmaids, all her pupils from the school – and Ella Ross shall make eleven – like the swans in the story.'

'Oh, I am glad you will stay!' Ella cried. 'You know Granda is now an old man. He may grow sick.'

'I shall look after him for you.'

'It is a load off my mind,' she said.

'But you must be happy, Ella,' he said gently. 'You never speak to Clement, though you were such friends, he says. He will live on the island and you will perhaps still be here. Will you never speak to him?'

She said in a low voice, 'My mother missed his father. Something happens, maybe. You grow and are older and other people come and everything is changed. It was all of a sudden different for her and now it is different for me.'

'Tell me how – how different?'

She shook her head. She could not have put it into words. She would have liked to tell him what she had often read – that all are equal in the eyes of God; or some such religious remark. But she could not quite remember the words she wanted, and anyway it was a bold thing to say, so she supposed; her mother would tell her so.

'Tell me – tell me!' he urged, his arm consoling, helpful.

'I canna.'

'Perhaps I understand. Yes, yes – I understand. One day it may be different, but it is not different yet ... That is a very hard thing to say to you, my dear Ella. But it shall never come between such friends as you and James Tremayne.'

She smiled – for speaking in that rather haughty manner he sounded as perhaps proud Granda might have sounded at his age. And there was, truly, already a hint of Innis Gharaidh in his speech.

The summer wore away and they were into September. Now the coarser heathers, many that John Maitland had reared himself, bloomed over the island, the later roses, the strange late lilies, that came from hotter climates. With the ending season came the ending holidays. Up at the house Ella, taken unwillingly to help, watched and handed stolidly while Margaret packed Clement's trunk for school.

'D'you mind my own mother did this for your father?' Margaret asked him.

'I never heard much about my father. I think, you know,

she didn't care to speak about him. But when she was here,' Clement said, 'the night before she left – she showed me where he fell.'

Margaret sat back on her heels.

'Well, now,' she said; and paused a moment. Then she went on folding and packing.

Ella felt her mother's surprise, even her pleasure, as keenly as her own. It was a slightly guilty surprise, as of two people who have not altogether understood a third.

That evening was Clement's last evening. Ella did not want to see him, and went as the light began to turn, to search for mussels on the shore. In spite of all this, it was no surprise to her to see Clement near the cave, as if waiting for her; nor did she turn and run away.

'I came to say good-bye to the place,' he said. 'It was a good time in some ways.'

She did not ask which ways, but walked beside him in silence along the tideline. The weather was changing. The long days of sunshine had misted a little and that evening was grey.

'I shall come back at Christmas,' Clement said. 'But perhaps you don't care about that, since you hardly speak to me these days.'

She spoke for the first time. 'You are someone else now,' she said.

He did not answer that. Instead he asked how the work would go now that they were short of a man.

'You know that my brother James loves the island already. He says he'll dig and work, just as my grandfather did.'

'But he will be mostly a doctor,' she said. 'So he tells me.'

'Oh, then – you know everything,' Clement said. 'I am quite disappointed not to be giving you news.'

'Hamish will come to help Granda,' Ella said. She spoke positively and knew it would be so, though nothing had been positively arranged.

'I see,' said Clement.

After that they were silent, walking on the shore. Then they turned and came back to the cave and it looked very clean and empty, as if he had never dwelt there so strangely all those days and nights.

'You must keep it for me until I come back,' he said.

She heard the echo and smiled at him for the first time. It was not a child's smile but a woman's. It was a smile of acceptance – yet of dismissal.

He surprised her then by fishing in his pocket and pulling out the little silver chain they had found in the rifled jewel box.

'You have it,' he said.

She owned nothing of the kind. It was pretty and it pleased her. It pleased her, also, because it was he who offered it. However, she shook her head.

'Why not?'

Not knowing quite what she meant, Ella said, 'Because it is a chain.'

'I see,' he said again. He put it back in his pocket, frowning. 'Why are you being proud? You are always proud these days.'

'We are both proud, maybe.'

He frowned, kicking at a shell, sending it spinning.

Ella said, 'Whisht!' in her mother's voice.

They both laughed; but sadly.

By the same time the next day he was gone. James had gone with him and would not return until the middle of next week. The house was closed. What was Miss Christabel feeling?

They sat over supper in the kitchen at home and nobody spoke much. Ella went out to shut up the geese. Then she paused, as she often did, looking out across the channel. The longest days were over. There were even two or three lights pricking the misty evening, like pinholes in paper shading a candle. The boats were out, quiet and familiar – Hamish and Alister in the new boat James Tremayne had said they must have at once.

As she had stood a thousand times in the place where she had been born, been a child and suddenly grown up, so Ella stood now, gazing upon familiar things. Only now, as she watched, the picture changed. She saw as she had never seen, heard as she had never heard. Over the island in the coming twilight the colours were muted of the garden that had grown to magnificence through the toiling years. The still grey of the sky had pulled the horizon to itself, so that the curving wall of the hemisphere arched over the whole world. Birds were on the move, travelling; the upper air was full of high and hidden wings. Nearer at hand, a missel thrush flew with its harsh demanding cry from the thorn bush where it had been feasting, then beat on strongly to the far side of the island before coming to rest. Insects moved, busy in the last minutes of day, the last days of plenty – there were a few bees, even, uneasy in the faint damp chill of the changed season.

Ella could have cried out at the joyous secrecy of what she almost understood – but she heard a familiar step behind her, a bit slower, the slightest shuffle.

'They have the new boat out, Granda,' she said, setting aside her own thoughts.

'Aye, so I see.' He paused beside her, looking across the water, quiet and steely. Then he said, 'Ella, lass, I have spoken with Mistress Maclean – about Hamish coming to work on Innis Gharaidh. She is willing. The money will be a great help, she says, and her sister's boy will give her the hand she needs.'

Ella said nothing for a moment.

'I thought you might be glad of it,' he said.

'I was thinking of Miss Christabel. She said he could be a scholar. It cannot please her that he wishes instead to be a gardener.'

'But he does wish, and therefore it is best for him. He has enough in his head of reason and good sense alone to make a good gardener. What he has of learning will not be wasted.'

'Will it not?'

'If I'd half the book learning that he has, I would have been twice the gardener! That is the truth, as God sees me.'

Ella smiled. She took his hand and drew him home. The geese were penned, the goats in their shed, the night now dropping down fast.

'It's damp, Granda. Come away in to the fire.'

'Read us a tale tonight, Ella, will you? It's a long day since you did so.' He pressed her hand warmly in his hard one. 'What shall you choose for us, this evening of autumn?'

'Oh,' she cried, 'anything! Anything! So long as it's not about the Laird and the gardener's granddaughter!'

He paused and put his arm round her, but fearing she might cry – though not for the reason he would suppose – she pulled away and ran on ahead.

Her mother looked up as Ella came in.

'Has Granda told about Hamish?'

'He has.'

Margaret paused. She looked at her daughter and there was something she needed to say but she could not quite get it out.

'He is a good lad,' she said. 'I am glad he will be coming.'

'I am glad, too,' said Ella. 'He is – truly a good lad.' In her turn she hesitated. Then she smiled slightly at her mother. 'And different enough,' she said.